ALSO BY LINDSAY HUNTER

Don't Kiss Me
Daddy's

UGLY GIRLS

UGLY GIRLS

LINDSAY HUNTER

Farrar, Straus and Giroux
New York

Farrar, Straus and Giroux
18 West 18th Street, New York 10011

Printed in the United States of America
Published in 2014 by Farrar, Straus and Giroux
First paperback edition, 2015

The Library of Congress has cataloged the hardcover edition as follows:
Hunter, Lindsay, 1980–
    Ugly girls / Lindsay Hunter. — First edition.
        pages   cm
    ISBN 978-0-374-53386-1 (hardcover) —
    ISBN 978-0-374-71012-5 (ebook)
    1. Friendship—Fiction.   I. Title.

PS3608.U5943 U55 2014
813'.6—dc23

                                        2014017266

Paperback ISBN: 978-0-374-53589-6

Designed by Abby Kagan

Our books may be purchased in bulk for promotional, educational, or business
use. Please contact your local bookseller or the Macmillan Corporate and
Premium Sales Department at 1-800-221-7945, extension 5442, or by
e-mail at MacmillanSpecialMarkets@macmillan.com.

www.fsgbooks.com • www.fsgoriginals.com
www.twitter.com/fsgbooks • www.facebook.com/fsgbooks

1   3   5   7   9   10   8   6   4   2

For you

UGLY GIRLS

PERRY AND BABY GIRL were in the car they'd stolen not half an hour before. A red Mazda. Looked fancier than it was, had to use hand cranks to put the windows down. Perry gathered it probably belonged to someone who wanted to look fancy but couldn't squeeze enough out her sad rag of a paycheck. Like how for years Myra, her mother, kept a dinged-up Corvette because it was red and a two-door. Couldn't even get the tiny trunk open without a crowbar. Then Jim came along with his logic and calm and sense and had it scrapped. Myra drove a mint-green Tercel now. Four doors. No dings.

Perry knew the Mazda was a woman's car 'cause of all the butts in the ashtray, all tipped with lipstick. Baby Girl had lit one up first thing, held it between her teeth, squinting through the smoke, cranked down the window so she could rest an elbow. Baby Girl with her half-shaved head, her blond eyelashes, her freckled arm resting on the steering wheel. *Fake-ass thug.* Sometimes it seemed mean thoughts were all Perry had for Baby Girl, but when she caught sight of herself in the side mirror she saw she was doing all the same shit.

They'd turned onto the busted-up highway, Baby Girl swerving like they were in a go-kart so the Mazda wouldn't get a flat. The rising sun the color of a pineapple candy, no more than a fingernail at the horizon. Not a single other car to be seen.

Baby Girl was muttering along with the music meandering out of the speakers. *You want some / you gonna have to take some / and I'ma get mine.* This was her favorite line. Her motto. She tried to make it Perry's also but Perry was not into that shit.

Perry was annoyed. Tired. Felt like her skin was turning to dough. Her legs and arms and heart, all starting to give in. The clock said 6:25 a.m. Eight hours and twenty-five minutes past when Perry said she was going to bed. She'd have to explain herself to Jim and Myra when she got home. She hated explaining herself, 'cause most of it was stuff she'd have to make up.

She'd meant to do right. She'd meant to stay in bed and fall asleep like Jim wanted, 'cause she liked Jim. But she made the mistake of opening her window, hoping it would cool her room down. All it did was let more hot air in, let her hear the quiet outside her window, the stillness she could not stand. The windows in the nearby trailers were mostly dark but for the flicker of a television, and it was like she had to do something, something other than turning out the light and closing her eyes and letting the night pass on by, like Myra. She had to make something happen.

And plus she'd got that text from Baby Girl. *Lets do this.* They had no plan. Just a general desire, like always.

It was easy to creep out of the trailer. Perry didn't even ease her window shut like she usually did. She knew Myra wouldn't be able to hear over her program, and Jim had gone to work his night shift at the prison. Even if Myra did hear, it was unlikely she would do anything about it. Just keep sipping her beer and snuggle down tighter under the covers.

Baby Girl had been standing by the pay phone at the Circle K. Her arms moving in that fluid way, heavy and slow, like she was thrashing underwater. She had her music on. When she saw Perry she yelled, "Wadup wadup?"

Baby Girl didn't care how people saw her. In fact, she wanted them to be afraid. Like how people used to act around Charles, only

worse. Once, the greeter at Walmart told them they had to leave if
they were just going to stand by the doors acting a fool and not buying nothing. "Suck my *dick*," Baby Girl told her.

The greeter lady went red, she held her hand to her mouth and
started crying. And Perry wished it was her who'd said it.

Baby Girl pulled her headphones down. Perry could hear a man
yelling *waka waka waka waka.* "I think we should go get us a ride,"
Baby Girl said, turned so Perry could see the slim jim sticking out of
her back pocket. Her brother, Charles, had made it out of a metal
coat hanger before his accident. They'd stolen it from him after.
Everything was before and after for Baby Girl now, Perry knew. Before the accident she'd talk about boys, and once Perry had walked
in on her doing sit-ups next to her bed. After Charles's accident it
was like Baby Girl did all she could to look hideous. Untouchable.

"Let's get a SUV this time," Perry said. She couldn't drive, knew
it was up to Baby Girl to choose what kind of car to get, but she'd
been wanting to sit up high like that.

"You are the show-offiest motherfucker I ever met," Baby Girl
said, but Perry knew it was a challenge she wouldn't say no to.

They went into the Circle K to get the usual. Hot fries and a sweet
tea for Baby Girl, Mountain Dew and Twizzlers for Perry. She liked
her heart to go go go all night long.

"Where you girls headed tonight?" the man behind the counter
asked. He was an Indian-looking man but he had an accent like theirs.
Dark and syrupy, twang twang twang. His name tag said Patel.

"Why would we ever tell you that, Patel?" Baby Girl flicked her
change, a nickel, across the counter. It hit the man in the zipper. "Oh
shit!" Baby Girl exploded with laughter, holding her gut and pointing, like some of the boys did in the hallways at school. "That'll keep
your ass honest!"

He shook his head, wiped at his pants like the nickel had left a stain. "You are a pretty girl," he said, chopping his hand at Perry. "You should be at home asleep in your bed with curlers in your hair."

Baby Girl laughed, a grinding dry kind of sound like she was pushing something out her throat. Something else she got from the boys at school. They were almost outside when he yelled, "Ain't nothing open past one a.m. but legs!"

Baby Girl laughed hard at that, too, but once they were outside her laughter got all swallowed up by the quiet of the night and then what was the point. Baby Girl put her headphones back on. They walked along the road, Baby Girl's arms moving fast, pointing, punching, hands forming signs only she knew the meaning to. Perry stepped on every crack she could see in the dark yellow of the streetlamps, something that felt like her own way of saying fuck you to no one.

The night was warm as a mouth. "I think we should hit up the Estates again," Baby Girl shouted. Her voice quieted the cicadas, but only for a second. Perry gave her the A-OK sign. Wanted to say, *Keep it down, dumb-ass*, but didn't.

The Estates was a ritzy-ass neighborhood with a gate at the front and open sidewalks on either side. Perry and Baby Girl had hit the neighborhood before, strolled right in. Those sidewalks were an invitation: Come on in, and steal some stuff while you're at it. Perry had started to think if rich people weren't afraid of their stuff being taken, they wouldn't feel so rich.

The last time they were at the Estates, they'd tried doors until they found one unlocked. It was a brick house with a duck wearing a dress next to the mailbox. The first floor was a maze, every room connected to the next. They'd walked around and around, losing and finding each other. There was a picture of an old man and woman holding hands at the beach. Another picture of the same couple in front of the house. Baby Girl took the gold napkin rings she found in a drawer. Perry almost took an old pair of baby shoes frozen in bronze, but then she saw the iron poker next to the fireplace and took that instead, kept it in a dresser drawer, under some T-shirts. Perry took it out once, aimed, brought it through the air like it was a sword. Tried not to feel stupid. Lately it was like Perry could feel stupid faster than she could feel afraid.

When they got to the gate, Baby Girl pulled her headphones down, turned off her music. Took a deep breath, like she was about to say something, but the chimes in Perry's phone sounded. "Turn that shit off!" Baby Girl hissed.

It was a text message from Jamey. *Perry, girlie, where are u? Im online.* Perry turned the ringer off, stuffed the phone back in her pocket.

"Okay," Baby Girl said. "Let's make a left at the stop sign instead of a right this time. And let's take the first SUV we see. These mother-fuckers all have two-car garages but someone's bound to have a third car stuck out in the driveway that we can gank."

She was right. In front of a yellow house with a rock garden instead of grass, there was a huge black Suburban. Baby Girl pointed up. Blue light gently flickered behind the white curtains in an upstairs window. Someone was awake watching TV, or had fallen asleep while watching it.

"It's *on*," Baby Girl whispered. She pulled the slim jim out, worked it into the door. The lock went with a soft *pop*. For Perry, that *pop* was an exploding cosmos of possibility. White tails of glitter shooting out. It felt like she and Baby Girl were mirrors reflecting the light from the streetlamps back and forth a million times. They were light. They could do anything, go anywhere. They were light. Tomorrow Perry would be tired, *wrung out* like Jim would say, but this was why it was worth it. Who else was out at this hour, doing what they were doing, marking every moment, trying to live? No one else. *Wake up!* she wanted to shout at the white curtains, at all the windows in this neighborhood. *Wake the* fuck *up*.

Baby Girl hot-wired the car, backed out of the driveway. And it was just like Perry thought being that high up would be. She felt as tall as a tree.

THE SUV WAS A STUPID IDEA. Too obvious. Baby Girl had read in one of her brother's old books how you had to build up your tolerance for fear until it became part of you, as natural and unassuming as your own hand. And how often did you think about your own hand? Not often. That's where you had to get with fear. But even so, building up a tolerance didn't have to mean doing dumb shit over and over.

"We should ditch soon," she said to Perry. "Don't you think any cop could drive by and wonder, 'Hey, why is this baldheaded bitch driving a truck that clearly don't belong to her?' "

"Whatever," Perry said. In the beginning she'd say stuff like *You ain't ugly* when Baby Girl said mean shit about herself. Now it was mostly *Whatever*.

"They'll probably accuse me of kidnapping you, too, since no pretty girl in her right mind would be associated with—"

"Fine, we can ditch. Okay? Let's ditch."

Baby Girl knew she'd ruined it for Perry. She was over there feeling like a queen high up in her seat and Baby Girl had broken the spell. She almost laughed, it felt like such a triumph. She wasn't as pretty as Perry, but she was meaner.

After Charles came out of his coma he was different. Sweeter. Not interested in going out once it got dark. His edges were dulled. It was sad to see. So Baby Girl took up where he left off. Went from

Dayna to Baby Girl, Charles's nickname for her before his accident. Shaved half her head. Took his CDs, even some of his clothes, not that he seemed to care. After the accident he just wanted to wear basketball shorts, probably because of the elastic waistband. Lately Baby Girl had been considering carving a scar into the bald part of her head like the one her brother had from his stitches, jagged and mean-looking, like a child had practiced writing an S there. Baby Girl wanted her outside to look like how she felt on the inside. Which was *Fuck you*.

Tonight she was wearing a pair of Charles's jeans, so huge on her that she had to cuff the bottoms three times, and what used to be his favorite black T-shirt. Sports bra to tamp those fuckers down. Work boots she'd stolen from Payless. Kicked them, box and all, out the door while the saleslady was in the kids' aisle. Pretended to consider the shoelaces for a while, then went on her way.

She always tried to feel a glimmer of regret. It was so easy to take advantage. Why did she have to be the type to take advantage? Well, she *wanted* those boots. That was the main thing when you got right down to it.

Plus lip liner and gloss. That completed her look.

Baby Girl's prettiest feature was her lips: plump and pink. She had watched tons of YouTubes featuring women who knew about makeup demonstrating what to do with lips like hers and had settled on the liner-and-gloss method. It called them into focus while maintaining their natural color. And it made her look like a tough bitch.

Perry looked like some kind of garden fairy, only tall. Bright green eyes, black eyelashes, blond hair. Tanned legs. Smallish boobs. Baby Girl was grateful that Perry wasn't entirely perfect: she had a widish nose, a fang on one side of her mouth, and way back, a gray molar. Fixable problems but only if you had the money for it. And

Perry didn't. But neither did Baby Girl. Which was an important level to share.

Tonight Perry wore her usual ponytail, the same shorts from yesterday, a yellow T-shirt. Sandals. Each toe with a chipped remnant of polish. Perry came off like she didn't give a fuck about stuff like that. Baby Girl had learned that that was usually the way with pretty girls.

They drove, windows down. Somehow this Suburban didn't have a CD player, or if it did, Baby Girl didn't know where.

"Let's get something to *drink*," Perry said, which meant she wasn't so pissed about ditching anymore. Baby Girl knew she meant something they could get shitty on. That meant going to the *other* Circle K, the one with the guy who sold to anyone.

"Okay," Baby Girl said, "but after that we got to dump this thing."

"Oh hell yeah," Perry said, attempting one of Baby Girl's signs.

"You can be a real fuckin' hillbilly sometimes," Baby Girl told her.

"Oh well," Perry said. Her other favorite comeback lately.

Baby Girl made a U-turn. Up ahead, she could see flashing lights. She gripped the steering wheel. Her heart thudded like bass turned way up.

But it was just a tow truck. In her headlights she saw a man with his hands to his head, a jagged spill down his shirt. The tow truck driver seemed to be ignoring him. "Yo, that guy is *wasted*," Baby Girl said as they passed.

Perry leaned up, pulled her phone out of her back pocket, studied it. She made a quiet noise, something like a snort, then put her phone back in her pocket. "Who keeps blowing your shit up?" Baby Girl asked.

"Just this guy," Perry said. "I don't even know him."

Perry's stepdad, Jim, was a prison guard. A quiet guy who seemed as big as a standing bear. Perry loved him, Baby Girl knew, but she also seemed dead set on making sure he had a heart attack. Once he saw Perry's phone bill he'd want to know who this guy was. Happened every time. It seemed like a luxury to Baby Girl, toying with that kind of love and concern. But she knew better than to say shit about it to Perry.

She waited until Perry was looking out her window again, then pressed the button on her phone to check for texts. Nothing. She had gotten used to something waiting there for her nearly every time she checked, but in the past couple of days, nothing. She had gone too far, of course she had. Quickly, she texted, *Hey, sorry if I acted like a stupid bitch. Miss talking to u.* The *u* was her way of speaking his language, reaching out. Corny-ass text speak that no one she knew used, except for him. Jamey. Thinking his name made her feel like she had to pee. That always happened when she felt excited. Or scared. She pressed SEND, pushed the phone way down into her pocket, so she couldn't easily get it out to check again in the next thirty seconds.

There was a small woman behind the counter at Circle K, not the usual stoner who'd sell to them, so Perry and Baby Girl wiped down the Suburban and left it there and walked into the neighborhood next to it. This time, Baby Girl wanted a car with a CD player. These nights weren't hardly worth it without a way to listen to her music. The few times Charles had taken her out at night, he'd turned up the music so loud she could feel it in her teeth. Windows rolled all the way down, which meant lots of nasty looks from old ladies, but they had it wrong. Charles wasn't trying to annoy no one. He was trying to share it with them. Share that feeling. Windows down, the hot night breezing in and out of the car carrying the scent of gasoline, orange blossoms, garlic, exhaust. Music saying exactly what was in his heart, and what was in Baby Girl's heart, too, which went beyond anything you could say with words, but if she had to try it'd be *Yes.* And that's why you could have it loud. No one needed to say a thing. So she'd be damn sure the next car she and Perry got had that CD player. Perry would probably pout since Baby Girl's music wasn't her kind of music. But she wouldn't say nothing, because she knew it wasn't up for discussion, and because Baby Girl wouldn't be able to hear her anyway.

MYRA WAS ALONE AGAIN. Jim off to work and Perry out her window hours before. Perry might think Myra didn't know she snuck out, but Myra always knew. The whole trailer rocked if you stepped through the threshold, so she could always feel it rock and bounce as her daughter pushed herself out the window. It was what girls her age did. She did it too, and her momma tried many times to stop her. Well, she had decided long ago she wouldn't be two-faced with her own daughter like her momma had been.

Tonight she had the itch. Nothing but reruns on the television, and a news program about a war in a country Myra had never heard of. She had allowed herself one slowly sipped beer. Tried to watch for a while, get some culture, but twice they showed a dead child limp in his momma's arms. Myra was just not up for that shit, not tonight.

With the TV turned off she could hear her neighbor two trailers down cooking dinner, the sizzle in the pan, him humming some kind of nonsense, the farting squirt of the ketchup. She supposed she could make some dinner, too, but what? The fridge held eggs, juice, relish, beer.

Beer. She had a shift at 5:00 the next morning, and more than that she wanted to show Jim that she could get through a night without that kind of help. So no. No more beer.

The thing of it was, much as she tried to deny it, ignore it, she hated Jim working nights. She'd always had trouble getting through a night alone; even as a child one stray thought could keep her up for hours, staring at the ceiling, her heart like a mallet and her limbs so stiff, like they were cast in stone. The whole rest of the house at peace. The loneliness of that kind of exclusion. The only thing that helped was climbing into bed with her sister, or lying on the hard floor next to her momma's bed, which she could only do if her momma wasn't entertaining.

So sleeping in a bed without Jim, that rarely happened. Unless beer.

Myra tried to fill these nights with little tasks. Clean the kitchen, dust the furniture, look up recipes on the Internet. In the mornings she'd list what she'd done for Jim, like, *See? I can do this.* But reaching the end of her list always made her feel worse. What did it matter that the tablecloth got ironed, that the washers on the faucet got tightened? Jim would be gone the following night, and the night after, and the night after.

So, beer.

Before she could think twice Myra was outside, the door clicking behind her. When she sat on the steps she felt the trailer sag. The air greasy with the smell of onions and meat, the neighbor making burgers, or maybe meat loaf. Humming his ABCs. Did Myra recall that he had a grandchild staying with him?

A man in a sleeveless shirt walked out from between two trailers across the way, stopped when he saw Myra. "Evening," he called. In the light from her neighbors' windows Myra could see that his shirt had a graphic of a swordfish bursting out of the water. *Ain't skeered,* the shirt said.

"Evening," Myra called back.

"Thought I heard raccoons," the man said. "I hate 'em."

Only now could Myra see that he had a BB gun by his side. If she had a dime for every time she ran into someone carrying a gun in this clump of trailers, she'd be one rich woman.

"No luck, huh?" Myra called.

"No luck," he answered.

"Well, they're harmless, really. Sometimes I appreciate how they eat trash, what with how many litterbugs we got around here."

"Harmless till you get bit," the man said, walking closer. He had a baby face, if babies could get stubble. And something wrong with his lip. When he was right in front of her Myra saw he had one of them cleft palates, the scar a white trail through the stubble, made him look even more like a baby. He leaned the gun up against Myra's trailer.

"I'm Pete," he said.

"Myra Tipton," she said, held out her hand for him to take. His was warm and a little moist, but not unpleasant. It was clear he wasn't no hard laborer.

"I only been living here the past couple months," he said. "I live with my momma, been helping her out while she's sick."

"Ain't that nice," Myra said. He put his thumbs through his belt loops, cocked a hip. It occurred to her that he might be wanting to sit, but the steps were only wide enough to seat one. Besides, what would she look like, scooting over to let this baby-faced man sit next to her, for all the world to see?

"Why you out here all alone?" the man asked.

Myra couldn't put her finger on why—something about the way he asked it—but she decided to lie. "Oh, I'm not all alone," she said. "My husband's inside, taking a shower."

"But you still out here alone," he said, cocking to the other hip.

Myra stood up. "You're right," she said. "I better get inside where I won't be all alone no more. Nice meeting you." She turned quick, tried to jog up the steps like everything was no big deal. She was reaching out for the screen door handle when her foot got twisted up in her housedress. Grunted as she fell on her knees.

The man was on her in a flash, pulling her up by her elbows, opening up her screen door and helping her to her own couch. Her knees throbbed, the steps were ribbed metal, she could feel the pain pounding in the palms of her hands, too.

The man stood before her, hands out like he might need to catch her again. She had to peer up at him, the ceiling fan light making a halo around his head, his face darkened by it. It hurt her eyes. "Miss Tipton," he said. "You all right? I was just joking with you, I ain't really asking why you were out there on those steps all alone. I sit on my momma's steps alone every night, for no reason at all."

There wasn't no shower running, no husband coming out to see what all the commotion was about. This man, this Pete, surely knew Myra had been lying. He'd left his gun outside, didn't even seem all that concerned about some trailer kid coming along and taking it away. This boy could be just what the doctor ordered in terms of making the clock go go go.

"Pete," she said. She lowered her eyes finally, addressing her question to his gut. "You want a beer?"

He sat down next to her with such force that the cushion she sat on jumped. She could see his face clearly now, and felt surprised all over again at the scar on his lip. "Well, heck yes!" he said. "I ain't skeered!"

Myra used her fists to push herself up from the couch. His momma hadn't cared for that scar right. It bubbled up like a grub worm. She felt half sorry for him and half disgusted. She grabbed two beers, making sure the bottles bumped against each other, because it was her favorite sound. She pushed the disgust away. She had to. Drinking the night away was no biggie if it was a social occasion. And this surely counted.

JIM GOT TO WORK feeling like he'd been wrung out. Before he left, Myra had seemed fidgety. Never a good sign. And Perry's TV was still on, which meant she was still awake, hadn't turned it off and rolled over to sleep. She'd be out the window quiet as a cat not an hour after he left, he knew.

He wanted to leave the house with his family tucked in and safe, doors and windows locked snug, leaving a warm presence that never cooled. Wanted to return to a home filled with the yellow light of morning, have his coffee, crawl in next to his wife, fall to sleep without a care.

That hadn't happened in a long while. Instead, he knew he'd come home to Myra's bottle still in her hand, the foamy bits dried to a film at the bottom, Perry's door closed, her bed empty. The trailer dank and dark, the sky overcast, no yellow light. The neighbor playing her polka music loud enough for her to hear despite her broken hearing aid.

And before that, a long shift at the prison, which always left him feeling like he hadn't showered in days, like behind every piece of good news there was a shiv-sharp piece of bad news.

Jim had a walker's shift that night. Already, seated comfortably in his truck, he could feel his bones ache like he was driving home after a shift, not driving toward one. *Kadoom, kadoom*, he'd have to walk the lengths of the cell block over and over, the hard rubber soles in his shoes never giving, not ever; he'd asked to be allowed to wear black tennis shoes instead but had been denied. And in a way he felt reassured by that. In prison, order was key. Allow one crack—moving to less formal, more giving shoes—and the whole thing would fold in on itself.

He pulled up to the small guard shack. The new guard leaned out, a young black man named Davie. He smiled and Jim saw he was missing the top right incisor. A child's smile, and a child's innocence in his eyes, too. Hadn't seen shit yet. Jim handed over his own ID, attempted a smile in return, though he was sure it looked like he was simply brandishing his teeth.

Or was it Davis? This was new—these blips in his mind where he wasn't sure what was what. The stresses of a teenaged stepdaughter, of a wife giving in to the urges she'd been able to convince herself didn't exist for a time. Not much room to store things like the gate man's name. Did it even matter? Would he fold in on himself because he couldn't remember Davie or Davis? The brim of the man's hat was stiff, unworn. Jim waved, drove through.

Every shift began the same: Sign in at one door, show your badge, ask after the man's family, pretend to listen. Say *Morning* if it was Phil. Next door, same thing, only open up your lunch pail and let the man paw through it. *How's Sharon? And the kids? Good, good. Yep, cheese and mustard today, all out of cold cuts.* Next door, hold out your arms for a pat down, ignore this man as he ain't really the chatty type. Store your lunch pail and wallet and cell phone and keys and pen, if you were dumb enough to bring one in, in your locker. Badge up, gun up, nightstick loose in your hand. Walk through the final door. You're in.

He had about five minutes before the next shift began, so Jim joined Clapp, the other walker, where he stood just inside the final set of doors. They couldn't go early; everything had to be timed just so, no cutting corners or schedule changes, or else why bother? From here they could see all the way to the other side; this part of the prison wasn't nothing but one long rectangle with forty rooms on each side— twenty on top and twenty on bottom. Metal staircases on both walls, metal because it was sturdy and because, Jim had come to believe, nothing in this place could be quiet or peaceful. Footsteps rang off the stairs day in and day out, and the metal amplified all the other noise, too.

The yard was a sorry place where the men could get some quiet, the yard like a clay baseball diamond pocked with weeds and ciga-rette butts. When it rained, the yard became a swamp; when it was hot the dirt felt like it had been cooked in the oven. The infirmary was off the cafeteria, and the hole was underneath the cafeteria, in the basement of the basement, or so the warden called it. When he first started, Jim wondered if the men in the hole could smell things cooking in the cafeteria above. He'd soon found out that all you could smell down there was what the men brought with them: sweat, breath, fear. Working the hole was just as much a punishment as having to live down there. You patrolled it in mostly dark; you listened to the men crying or yelling or, worse, not making any sound at all.

Jim nodded at Clapp. He was a scrawny man, jumpy. Myra would say he looked rode hard and put up wet. He loved inmate gossip, and it seemed like every time Jim worked with the man he had a story.

"Hey," Clapp said. He was fiddling with a button on his cuff, couldn't quite get it to go through the eyehole. He stopped suddenly, put his hands on his hips, and Jim knew he was in for another story. "You hear Carver pulled a balloon of coke out an inmate's anus?" He peered at Jim, like Jim was the warden and could do something about it.

"You don't say," Jim said.

"Mm-hmm. Says he heard some talk so he did a strip search. Said it was bright green. The balloon was, I mean."

Jim waited. More and more, these kinds of exchanges felt like torture. He just wanted them to be over so he could get started on his shift, one second closer to it ending.

"Well, what do you have to say about that?" Clapp asked.

"I guess I'm not all that surprised," Jim said. Every day it was something. Stories abounded. O'Toole ate a prisoner's dinner every night for a month, right there in front of him, because the prisoner called his wife a whore.

"Right out the man's *asshole*," Clapp said, smacking his hands together, as if to wake Jim up. Now Jim wondered if the meaningful part to Clapp wasn't the smuggling of cocaine, but the fact that Carver had fiddled with another man's area.

"Good for Carver," Jim said. "I hope he wore gloves."

"Haw," Clapp howled, and some of the inmates in their cells mimicked him. Clapp wheeled, yelled, "Shut the FUCK UP." He put a hand to his ribs, shook his head. Six months ago Clapp had slipped on a tooth and fell down the stairs, right onto his nightstick. Broke two ribs. *Whose tooth?* Jim had asked when O'Toole told him the story. *Does it matter?* came the answer. Clapp went back to fiddling with his button, nodded at Jim, and walked toward the metal staircase on the right. They'd switch sides halfway through, take their breaks separately. This was all the human interaction there'd be, aside from whatever the inmates had in store.

O'Toole was known as a hardass. Clapp had a hair trigger. Jim wasn't sure what the other guards, or the inmates for that matter, said about him. Maybe, Jim Tipton once broke up a fight by throwing a hot pot of gravy onto the prisoners. Or, Tipton brought in his guitar and sang on Easter. Or, Tipton's wife used to call the front desk drunk and ask to talk to Jim, which wasn't possible during a shift, or asked when was Jim coming home.

Jim clanged up the steps. Men pretended to busy themselves, watching him from the sides of their eyes. Walk from one end to the other, turn, walk back toward the other end. Go down the stairs, walk that end to end, too. He knew whatever floor he wasn't on, the men in their cells were up to something. Making dice out of soap, sharpening toothbrushes, coughing or howling in one cell so the guard would be distracted from what was happening in another cell, whispering plans so low it was a miracle anyone heard. Even if they were just lying there thinking, they were up to something.

"Hey," he heard a man say. "Hey, Tipton?"

It was a newer prisoner, only been inside eight months or so, a child-toucher named Herman. Some guards made it a point to ignore any names, to refer to the prisoners only by their numbers, but Jim wasn't like that.

Jim walked over to his cell. Herman had one blind eye that tended to roll around, making it hard to take him serious. Child-touchers had it rough in prison. Jim expected him to ask for more protection, or to see the warden, or even just to shoot the shit a little, make himself feel human for a while. "Speak," Jim told him.

"Oh, hey, Tipton." He aimed his good eye at Jim. "You got a daughter?"

Jim knew that prisoners were the most bored human beings on earth. Aside from forming gangs and working out and smuggling drugs and carving paraphernalia out of soap and having sex with each other and themselves, they loved to find ways to fuck with a person. It's about control, triumph. This was something Jim understood. A man wearing a jumpsuit and shuffling around in plastic shoes and getting bent over if he ain't watching close needs to find a way to stay a man. It was a truth that rang clear as a bell across the countryside.

Still, Jim stabbed his nightstick through the little slot in the door, right into Herman's good eye. The prisoner lurched back, fell to the floor with his hands cupped over his face, sobbing like he was a boy after his first punch.

"Don't you fucking ask me that again," Jim said. He'd make sure the man saw a doctor, it's what separated him from some of the other guards, and he didn't often hit the prisoners. It's just that from time to time that bell rung true for him, too.

WHEN SHE WAS YOUNGER, about Perry's age, drinking with her friends made the nights feel plump with possibility. The way the streetlights could blur, the way music was never loud enough, the highway going east forever in one way and west forever in another. Even sitting in someone's garage waiting around for something to happen—there was always the guarantee that something would happen. What could the future hold? It didn't matter, as long as there was that feeling.

Myra felt that way now. Her body warm and relaxed, the pleasant yellow light of the living room, the whole world outside the trailer for her to join or ignore. A new friend two cushions over, the sting in her hands and knees just a dull throb. What could be wrong with trying to preserve that feeling?

"You should put up some twinkle lights," Pete said.

"You think?" Myra was tickled. Such a young-person thing to say, and he was saying it to her like nothing. "Where, up around the television?"

"Maybe," he said. "Or lining your windows. White ones, though, not them multicolored ones. Those are tacky."

"You're right." Myra held her beer to her knee. It'd be swollen but the beer was cold enough to help that a little. If Jim didn't want her to drink, why didn't he pour it out, get rid of it, yell at her some? Jim just wanted her to be happy, that's why. The thought made her feel safe. Loved. Maybe she'd do a little something for him. Make him a pot roast. A sandwich, at least.

Pete took a swig from his bottle. Myra loved that sound, that clean sound of the beer coming down the neck. He held his fist to his mouth, belched. But a quiet belch. Polite.

"You know," he said, "I've seen you before."

"Oh?" Myra didn't like this. When had he seen her? When she was dressed for work? That'd be okay. Or when she was passing by her windows in her robe, red-eyed, hair all messed up, hungover? That would not be okay.

"Yep. I seen you and your daughter one day. Coming home from somewhere. You both looked pissed off." At this he laughed a little, into his fist again.

"Yeah, that's us all right," Myra said. She took a drink, held the bottle to her other knee. "She's a handful. You remember being a teenager?"

"Course I do. Wasn't *that* long ago for me."

He finished off his beer, his throat moving with each pull. Myra had said something wrong, had passed him an oar in the "Ain't we old?" boat.

"No, no, that ain't what I meant," she said. "I know you're still a young man. I just meant there's a difference between your teenage years and your adulthood."

"I get you," he said.

Myra pushed herself up, limped into the kitchen to get more beer. "Of course," she said, "it's important to maintain some stuff from your teenage years." She spoke to him across the tiny bar in between the kitchen and the living room. He didn't turn his head toward her. What was she doing, talking to this strange person about being a teenager? "That excitement," she added, "you know what I mean?"

He grunted, grunted again when she handed him a fresh beer.

Myra lowered herself back onto the couch. After a while he said, "I didn't have the most fun teenage years."

Myra waited for him to go on, but he just took a swig and sat there. "Well," Myra said, "I'm sorry to hear that."

"Nice of you to say."

"Me, I had a great time in high school. Back then everybody hung out with everybody. There wasn't no cliques. Football players wouldn't just go for the cheerleaders, if you get me. And I wasn't no cheerleader."

The beer was making her chatty. She could feel her mouth getting away from her, wanted to stop, but it felt too good, saying these things. Remembering.

"One time I—"

"Your daughter ain't no cheerleader, either, am I right?"

She had been about to tell him about the time she had drag raced from one stoplight to another, one of those spur-of-the-moment events she treasured. She had won, had kissed the boy she'd raced full on the mouth right there in front of his girlfriend, that's how filled with triumph she'd been. He had tasted like eggs and she had come to know that most mouths tasted like eggs when they were caught off guard like that. She was overcome with the memory of that night, that moment, her heart pounding, her mouth still open like she was going to keep right on talking, but Pete's question had caught up with her, frozen her.

"No, she doesn't cheerlead," Myra said. "How you know that?"

"Well, like I said, I seen you before. And I ain't never seen her in no cheerleader's uniform."

Was he making small talk? Why interrupt her story like that? Was she being a glory days bore?

"Uh-huh," Myra said. "Nope, she's not the peppy type."

"Me neither," he said. "Or I mean, I wasn't the peppy type, back when I was in school. Do y'all get along? Fight a lot?"

"We get along fine," Myra said. "We fight sometimes, but that's normal."

Myra knew what was going on. She'd overplayed her hand, taken this young man for a confidant, this man closer to her daughter's age than her own. Now he was making polite conversation, was about two questions away from saying, *Well, I better get going.*

"She seems like a real spitfire," he said.

"You could say that," Myra said. Took in two gulps of her beer. That'd be a burp, one she'd be hard-pressed to hold in, guaranteed.

"Where's she at?" he asked.

"Oh," Myra said, "I don't know. Out for an evening stroll, is what she told me."

"You don't seem too worried about her. What if she ain't out for a walk? What if she's out doing wrong? Or tied up in some maniac's closet?"

Already Myra was thinking of the bath she'd take, how she'd pour a beer into a glass and take it with her, light a candle, maybe even fall to sleep in the tub for a while. Who was this Pete, asking her about her parenting?

"That's on her," Myra said. "She knows right from wrong."

They looked at each other. Myra saw how his cleft lip made it difficult to keep his lips shut all the way, how his eyes moved quick, taking everything in, green but for a big brown spot in the right one. Finally he looked away.

"Well," he said. "I better get going."

Myra almost shouted *Aha!*, she was so pleased with herself for calling it.

"Thanks for the beers." He got up, smoothed down his jeans, straightened his shirt. Such pride, Myra thought, in his rags. It felt good to think it.

"Stop by anytime," she told him, tipped her beer. She felt surprised to realize that she meant it.

At the door he turned and said, "You think about those twinkle lights."

"I will," Myra said, the screen door snapping to.

She listened to see if he remembered to take his gun. Only now did she realize she'd been aware of it out there the whole time, keeping her mind tuned to it like she would if it was a feral cat that could speak her name. Like it might grow legs and walk in, right up to her, and spit in her face.

THEY ROLLED THE RED MAZDA out of the gravel driveway. The owner had left the keys balanced nice and sweet on the back left tire. A gift. Baby Girl listened to the same GBE song again and again, like she was trying to convince herself she was as bold as the hard thumping beats rattling the windows, like her tank was empty and she was filling it right back up. The bass was so loud it made the car feel like a vise, squeezing tighter with each beat. What Perry wouldn't give for a song featuring an actual instrument.

They stopped for French fries at Denny's. Baby Girl went to the bathroom, came back with her lip liner refreshed, looking to Perry like a batty old lady who forgot to fill her lips in. It had started a few months ago, this outlining, and Perry never got the nerve to tell her. Baby Girl had pale red hair, orange really, the same color freckles, no eyelashes to speak of, and blue eyes set against a lightningscape of red. A body best described as *solid*. Baby Girl showing evidence of any kind of vanity was a miracle and so Perry left it be.

"Yo, can we get some menus?" Baby Girl called out.

A waitress in a short brown wig wheeled around from where she was taking a man's order. Two penciled brows looking like wobbly cartoon frowns above her eyes. "In a *minute*," she snapped. The man had a mesh hat balanced atop his head, dark tinted glasses. Thin frowning mouth like his was penciled in too.

Baby Girl had her mouth open like she was about to say something back, but Perry didn't feel like starting. "Shoot, try me?" Baby

Girl muttered. She had decided it wasn't worth it, was letting it go, and Perry felt her body sag a little in relief. Her eyes felt dry as rocks. She was starting to long for her bed earlier and earlier lately.

A boy with a mop and bucket appeared, pushing through the doors from the kitchen. Perry recognized him from her math class. Short blond hair, strong arms, brown eyes. A boy her momma would call *real clean-cut* the same way someone else would say *This steak is nice and juicy.* Perry had once dreamed about him. She was chasing him through a forest, holding a spear. Myra would have liked that. She put a lot of faith in what dreams could tell a person about her life, but Perry had always felt that dreams were just random collections of stuff that bored you plus stuff that quaked your soul with desire or shame.

"Travis," she called to him, before she even realized she knew his name.

Baby Girl turned around to see who she was talking to. "Oh *shit*," she said under her breath. "You think he saw the Mazda?"

Perry ignored her. She had to peel her thighs off the vinyl booth seat, and as she walked over to talk to him she wondered if they were red, if they looked like she had sat on the toilet for too long. She wished she hadn't had the thought, knew she must look bright red as well as sweaty to him. Did she care? That was the question.

"Oh, hey," Travis said. He looked at her like it took all he had to allow his eyes a glance.

"I didn't know you worked here," she said.

"Oh yeah," he said, looking around, like he'd just remembered where he was. "Trying to make some money." He stared at his shoes, black plastic clogs.

"Nice shoes," Perry told him.

"I have to wear these," he said quietly, like she had accused him of something. But Perry had just wanted to make him laugh. "No," she said, "they really are nice." It came out sounding even meaner.

She had that thing where the sweeter she tried to sound, the more it came off like bullshit.

"Nice seeing you," he said, and pushed his mop into a roped-off part of the dining room. He had a bleach stain on the back of his shirt the shape of a splattered kidney.

Perry walked back to the table. Baby Girl had been watching the whole thing, her face split in two, dead eyes, wide grin.

"Damn," Baby Girl said, "that guy thinks you're a bitch."

Perry watched Travis push the mop, back and forth, truly cleaning. He was a hard worker, it was clear. She knew if it was her with the mop she'd push it back and forth a couple times and call it a day. But if he was watching her she'd try harder, if only to make him think she could work hard like him. She cared what he'd think of her, suddenly there it was, put in front of her like a plate of pancakes. She could feel the spear in her hand, the warmth heading south. She wondered did her lips look dry, did she have sleep crusted in her eyes, did she look ugly to him?

He never once turned to look at her, just pushed the mop right through the swinging doors to the kitchen.

The waitress came over, staring at her pad instead of at them. They ordered without menus because all they wanted was French fries, and because the waitress wasn't offering menus anyway. Baby Girl made a point to use her name. "And some ranch for dipping, *Pam*." She always went the extra mile to give someone shit. Which, Perry realized, made her the Travis of assholes, only instead of a mop she had her mouth.

Denny's was always where it all caught up with her. She could feel exhaustion closing over her like a heavy drape. It was the sitting still, the eating, the bright lights. Travis still hadn't come back out from the kitchen. Perry wondered if he was the one doing the cooking. Did he spit in the fryer, like she would have done? She found herself hoping he had.

They left the waitress two quarters for a tip. Baby Girl fixed them to the table with a wad of gum that had been chewed colorless. In the parking lot she was chewing again, always obsessed with the smell of her breath. Perry didn't know how she could be so concerned with her breath and so unconcerned with the goblin she kept drawing on her face.

The Denny's was just a short coast off the highway, and they had to talk loud to hear each other over the roaring inhale and exhale of traffic. "One more?" Baby Girl asked. Already her lip was beaded with sweat, and it made her look like a child who'd just taken a sloppy drink of something. Perry shook her head so she wouldn't have to yell. She wanted to go home but knew Baby Girl wasn't ready, knew they'd need to drive the Mazda up the highway, back down it, like two dummies trying to get a screeching baby to sleep. A screeching Baby Girl.

They drove over to the Walmart to do doughnuts in the employee parking lot. Baby Girl had once filled out an application to work there. They'd gone in to check on the status later that week and Baby Girl told the greeter to suck her dick. Now her applying for the job had become a joke, something she laughed at when telling the story, like she never really meant it. But Perry knew she had meant it, had worn nice black pants and a white blouse to apply. With Baby Girl it was two steps forward and a day's worth of walking backward.

Baby Girl parked but left the keys in the ignition. Always ready to take off again. She walked slow with her hands in her pockets, shoulders hunched, staring at the ground, drifting in and out of the headlights' glare. Every now and then she bent to pick up a bit of newspaper, crumpled receipts, a palm frond gone brown. Kindling for the small fire Perry knew she was fixing to make. Dumped it all in one of the carts left outside, held her lighter to the palm frond, which took to the fire like that was all it was waiting for to look alive again. Bright orange rib cage of a thing, quickly turning black. "Shit!" Baby Girl hissed, and ran back to the car.

Perry watched the tiny curls of flame for as long as she could as they drove off. Myra was always talking about itches, how people were either scratchers or ignorers. The scratchers poke and poke at it, even though it makes it itch more. The scratchers love the itch and they love the poking. It could go on forever but for the blood, and even then, it's a small price to pay. That's how nights with Baby Girl had gotten. None of it seemed to matter. The sun always came up.

They ditched the Mazda on the side of the highway, near the exit headed back to where they'd left Baby Girl's car on a quiet street. Cars rushed by them as they walked along the shoulder, some honked, people on their way to work or home from work, probably none of them on the way back from an all-night bender like they had been on. Baby Girl made a visor of her hands to protect her face. She was so pale that even ten minutes in the sun could do her in. Even a weak sun like this one, set back behind a screen of gray. Even this sun would turn her red as a fire ant. "See you at school," she said.

Perry nodded, turned down the road leading to her house. She was too tired to say anything back. She had to walk while Baby Girl got to drive home because she couldn't risk Myra hearing the car, or worse, Jim seeing it on his way back from work.

Baby Girl honked as she rode past. Trying to get a rise. Perry ignored her, concentrating on how hard the asphalt felt under her feet. Every step a pounding. She walked through a few neighborhoods on her way to the trailer park, each dingier than the last, until she got to one of the nicer ones, brick homes with actual grass in the yards, no cars parked on the street, a man in a suit taking a mug of coffee to his car. Next would come the cul de sac of duplexes and apartments, pretty yellow siding and flower boxes, though the parking lot out front had cracks and potholes, and there weren't any BMWs or Lexuses, just Nissans and Hyundais and maybe a Buick or two. Then there was the neighborhood of short, squat houses, skinny driveways, no sidewalks, shrubs and grass looking like they'd gone months without seeing to. Mostly old trucks parked out front, sometimes rickety-looking motorcycles. And finally her own neighborhood, if it could be called that, short rows of trailers leading up a small hill. Hers was three rows back. Perry knew what people thought when they heard the words *trailer park*. Dirty kids in dirty diapers, car parts, people drinking or hollering. But that wasn't so true for where she lived. They had all those things, but never all at once, it seemed. And if you had a double-wide, like Myra and Jim did, it almost felt like a normal-size house. Perry didn't love it, but it was home.

It was nearly seven thirty when she got there. Myra was still in bed, either because she had a day off or because she didn't wake up when her alarm went off. Perry knew it was probably the second option, what with her having a beer last night. No telling how many came after.

The trailer was quiet and still; it felt to Perry like the preserved remains of a family long gone. Myra collected things, little colonies of shit, and displayed them all over the trailer. Along the windowsill behind the couch she had her group of vintage glass jars; dust had coated them long ago, so instead of reflecting light they just distilled it, held it like a glaze. The couch had its own grouping of pillows, embroidered with dog heads or sayings like COFFEE MADE ME DO IT and IT'S 5 O'CLOCK SOMEWHERE. Mostly pillows Myra picked up from the truck stop. They helped hide how worn the couch was, all its rips and tears, same went for the doilies Myra collected. The walls of the trailer were faux wood paneled, so cheap you couldn't drive a nail through to hang up a school photo without the whole wall splitting and your picture frame falling to the floor in a shatter. Myra had grouped photos on top of the TV, on the floor in front of the TV, and on the bar leading into the kitchen. None of Perry past the age of eight, like time had stopped once Perry went into the fourth grade. Jim and Myra's wedding photo in a huge scalloped frame, Myra in a pink pantsuit and Jim in a stiff white shirt, perched on the back of the easy chair against the wall. If you sat too hard it'd topple, and they had all learned how to sit just so, all learned to lean their heads back to hold it in place, all learned you sat in that chair as a last resort. It wasn't like they all sat together much anyway, so there was usually plenty of room on the couch. Between the couch, the chair, the TV on its stand, and all the shit Myra arranged everywhere, there was about a two-foot path from the front door to the hallway off the bedrooms. Just enough to get by.

When Myra started bringing stuff home, Perry knew she was trying her hardest not to drink. And it worked, but it also held her feet to the fire. A constant reminder of the distraction she craved.

Jim would be pulling up soon to take Perry to school. She showered, mussed up her bed to make it look like she'd been in it. Maybe he wouldn't know, though he probably would, but even so, Perry knew it was important to at least pretend for him. She got on the computer while she waited, listening for his truck.

There was a message from Jamey.

NO SUBJECT.
Perry girlie,
It has been a lonley nite without you. I got to turn in soon becos I have school in the morning. I guess so do you. Maybe your asleep??? Anyways, hope to talk to you tonite.
Jamey

It was a thrill having a friend like this, a friend Perry could pretend with when there came a need, but it was also a lot of work. Jamey had added her on Facebook months back, and she'd finally accepted his request on a night when Baby Girl couldn't go out. His profile said he went to high school a few towns over. He played baseball and was all right looking from what Perry could tell.

Now he wanted to talk every single night. She had given him her phone number but he never called, just texted, because he had free texting but limited minutes. Part of Perry was waiting for the other shoe to drop, to find out it was Baby Girl or some jerk from school playing a joke.

In the meantime, it was fun to read what he had to say, especially when it got sexual, and it usually did. *Ooooh baby*. He loved to write that line. *Ooooh*. It almost got her to feel sorry for him.

Perry had been hoping the message was from Travis. Seeing Jamey's message instead, seeing his need to talk to her, it was a *need*, bared naked and misspelled in a dumb Facebook message, it turned her stomach. Even worse was the fact that she had her own need, a need for Travis to like her, and she wasn't no better than Jamey.

She looked away from the computer, away from Jamey's message. The lumpy couch, the worn quilt covering the threadbare patch in the arm, the crocheted rug beaten nearly white over the years, the endless, endless army of glass figurines posing across every flat surface. The house felt empty despite the three people living in it. Myra filled it with stuff and more stuff.

Every time she got to thinking like this it was like time stopped and froze her right where she sat. She'd never leave this shabby, unloved room. The Perry that she was right then, that girl was trapped forever. Before she knew it she had a glass figurine of a rearing horse under her shoe, using her full weight to mash it into the linoleum. Why had she said that thing about Travis's shoes?

Then again, why had he acted like such a bitch about it?

She swept up the shattered horse, buried it under some paper towels in the trash can. At least six bottles in there, probably more around Myra's bed. That answered that. She went back to the computer.

Jamey had left a comment on her newest profile picture. *Haha your beatifull even with that hat on!!* She had read one of Travis's papers once during a group activity in English. He was a good speller.

Outside, Jim pulled up, honked once. Ever since he found out Perry had skipped a few times, Jim didn't allow her to take the bus. "Jim, let her find her own way," Myra had said, "trust me." Perry could hear them through the wall. "Not when it comes to this," Jim said. The next day, he'd driven her to school. And all the days after that.

Which didn't mean Perry wasn't still skipping. But at least Jim felt better.

PERRY'S HAIR WAS WET, she was neatly dressed, she had her book bag. Jim knew if he checked she'd have made it look like her bed was slept in, had probably even punched a dent into her pillow, but the deep purplish lines under her eyes told a different story. He knew she hadn't slept at all.

She got into the car riding a wave of gray morning light. When the door shut, the light was gone. He felt sad about that, which meant he was just as exhausted as she must have been. "How was work?" she asked, but immediately turned her head to watch herself in the side mirror.

He wanted to tell her how he'd watched an inmate swallow mouthfuls of his own bright blood after he got in a fight with his roommate over toilet rights. Just gulp, and then his mouth would fill again, and then gulp. How Jim had held a roll of toilet paper up to the man's mouth and it got half soaked. But he knew he'd never say things like that to her, and he knew it wouldn't matter if he did.

Instead, in his usual quiet way, he said, "It was fine. Glad it's over. How was your night?" He said it in an *I know you weren't in bed not one single second* kind of way.

"Fine, glad it's over," Perry answered.

Now what did that mean, Jim wondered. Was she being cute? Or was she in trouble? But of course she was.

"You see your momma this morning?" Jim asked.

"Sure didn't," Perry said. "She was still in the bedroom with the door closed when I came—when I got up."

Jim let the slip go. "I'll check on her when I get back," he said. "I probably forgot to set her alarm."

They sat in silence the rest of the way there, and Jim was grateful for it. The prison was an ocean of sound. If you worked one of its cinder blocks out of the wall and held it up to your ear you'd hear waves and waves of men—men shouting, crying, moaning. After that, even silence was a roar.

"Hey," he said. "You want McDonald's?" This was something they did on special occasions. Fridays. Or when Perry got a good grade. This morning was the opposite of a special occasion, but that seemed to Jim even more of a reason than a B+.

"Hell *yes*," Perry said. She finally turned and looked at him. He could see what she'd look like as a grown woman: still pretty, but worn. Like a lily left on a tabletop for too long. Her green eyes were red in the corners. Then she smiled a little, her funny tooth resting on her lower lip, and she looked like a kid again. He filled with love for that kid.

"I could eat a whole hog," she said.

"Don't say hell," Jim said.

WHEN MYRA FIRST STARTED bringing Jim around, Perry thought he was some kind of scary giant who'd crush her like a soda can under his fist. This was after Myra's other boyfriend, Donald, had finally gone on his way. Donald was a scary toothpick type who'd crushed her with his mean mouth and his needle teeth and his beer breath.

But Jim was different. Looked Perry in the eyes the whole time she'd be talking. Cooked dinner, brought Myra flowers. Cheesy red roses, not a lot of creativity there, but it's the thought like they say. And he never drank. Perry was eleven when he came around, twelve when they got married. They moved into his trailer because it was a double and in a nicer park than the one they'd lived in before, an old Airstream with a single cot Perry slept on while Myra lolled on the two-cushion loveseat. He had a little garden out front, mostly strawberries and forget-me-nots, and he and Myra hung a wheel of chimes outside their window to christen the occasion.

Those chimes didn't last. It was like Myra didn't realize they'd make music every time a breeze blew by. They were gone after a week. And Jim's calm didn't fix her shit. She'd still miss a shift about once a week at Byron's Truck Stop—where she made doughnuts and sold truckers and teenagers their gas—because she'd be doing her drinking.

Perry tried to feel lucky that Myra didn't drink all the time, just some of the time, tried to feel lucky that even when she did drink she kept it tidy. No public scenes, no weeping calls from a bar like

Donald used to do. Myra just goes to her and Jim's room and drinks in bed till she don't know what's what.

Perry knew it was because of a sadness of some kind, or a noise she didn't want to hear. She had tried to get to the bottom of it, pin down the reasons why, but the truth was there was no list of reasons, unless that list included *everything* and *everybody*.

Myra had taught Perry about makeup and clothes and hair. Took care of her when she was sick. Smelled like Oil of Olay (her night cream) and limes (her Coronas). Once Baby Girl had called her a *drunk-ass drunk* and Perry socked her dead in her arm. Had meant to get her on the chin. It was the last thing Baby Girl ever said about Myra, and in return Perry stopped doing her impression of Charles in front of the TV.

Perry loved Myra the way any child loves their mother, only she could see her mom more clearly than just any daughter could. Myra wasn't some smeary presence who lived only for her kid. Perry was just a midpoint on her timeline. It was similar to how Perry saw Baby Girl. Both of them had their flaws, but Perry had her own, too.

She and Jim didn't have that same understanding, but that was a good thing. Jim wanted Perry to hold on tight to her innocence until she arrived safely into adulthood. It was nice to be seen that way, like she was unsmudged and unwrinkled and flapping dry in a clean spring air. Until someone pulls the pins and what, it's time to lay flat on a bed? Was that what adulthood was? If so, she'd been an adult since she was fourteen.

Jim pulled into the Walmart parking lot so they could turn around and go back toward the McDonald's. It was strange seeing it in the light of day, knowing she and Baby Girl had just been thugging there not hours before. Perry almost wanted to ask Jim could he drive around back, just real quick. She wanted to see the tire marks from the doughnuts. The embers from the fire. Had it actually all happened? It seemed like a dream she'd feel dumb for having.

WHEN BABY GIRL GOT HOME Charles was eating Cheerios out of a mixing bowl. "This is good," he told her. She could see the open bag of sugar on the table in front of him, a ladle sticking out of it. No wonder it was good.

"Hey, Charles," she said, "you make some for me?"

"Oh my Lord," he said. This was his new thing. *Oh my Lord.* He had gotten it from their uncle Dave, who they lived with, and who had found God after Charles got hit by a car while on his motorcycle a little over a year ago. Dave had been out all night that night, which used to be common, had come home to a police officer waiting in his driveway. Ran right to church after that. Baby Girl could understand. Church answers a lot of questions for you, so you don't have to yourself. Back in the day she used to go to church and it wasn't all that bad, she played bells in the kids' choir, ganked Danishes to eat with her little friends before Sunday school, bowed her head to pray to a God she imagined looked like Santa Claus in his pajamas.

Church just didn't intersect all that cleanly with her interests these days, was the thing.

"Dayna," Charles said, "I forgot to make you some. This is all that's left. The box is *empty*!" He handed it over, which was exactly what Baby Girl wanted him to do. When Charles ate too much sugar he crashed hard.

"Go get in the shower," she told Charles. "Hurry up, 'cause I got to get in there after you." She pointed at her hair with the cereal spoon. "My shit's all kind of nappy."

"You look beautiful," Charles said. He worked his finger into a nostril. "You're my sister!" He wiped his finger on the tablecloth.

"That's fuckin' gross, Charles," Baby Girl said, but she was laughing. This new Charles had no shame. Walked out of his room naked, ate tubs and tubs of ice cream, loved giving high fives, told Baby Girl he loved her, she was beautiful. The old Charles wouldn't be caught dead digging in his nose, wouldn't be caught dead in basketball shorts, ate healthy, had tons of girls blowing his cell up day and night.

The old Charles also used to steal cars and deliver them to someplace or other to be stripped for parts, used to carry a gun. Baby Girl took the gun from him after he came home from the hospital, after he held it up asking, *Is this real?* It was in an old shoebox under her bed, wrapped in paper towels and duct taped.

Charles stood up, pulled off his shirt. "Do I have time for a bubble bath?" he asked.

"Hell no you don't," Baby Girl said. "You got time for a *shower* like I *said*."

Charles kicked his chair over. This was another part of the new Charles. Whatever he was feeling, he made sure it was obvious. He had come at Baby Girl a few times, charging, but if you waited him out he usually calmed down or got distracted.

Baby Girl stared at the upturned chair, her eyebrows raised. Charles was breathing hard.

"Remember how you like the shower, 'cause it's like that time you ran around in the rain?" Baby Girl asked.

"Oh," Charles said. "Oh yeah!" He pulled his shorts down, ran to the bathroom, kicking them off as he went.

Baby Girl exhaled. She was gripping the spoon still, there was the bass in her heart again. Charles, if he wanted to, could do some damage.

But so the fuck could she. She took a bite of the Cheerios. Gagged. The only crunch left was from the sugar. She checked her phone again, and her heart thudded quick and heavy, because this time there was a text. How she'd missed it she didn't know.

U online?

She ran to the desk, where Dave's PC sat like an old car waiting to be scrapped. Took forever to boot up, took forever to get online. Baby Girl imagined Jamey waiting, drumming his fingers, jiggling his knee just like she did when she felt impatient, then giving up right as Baby Girl finally made it online.

But he hadn't given up. She saw his name right there in her buddies list. *Available.*

Hey, she wrote.

Well hey urself

Baby Girl smiled, because it seemed like she'd been forgiven, and because it was such a strange thing to say. No boy she knew talked like that. Cheerful, playful. Flirty, maybe, if she let herself think that far.

Where u ben u usualy always online wen I wana talk

Baby Girl felt indignant, even though it was true, she *was* usually online these days, waiting for him. But he was acting like it was her fault they'd stopped talking.

She didn't used to go online all that much, it felt vain and desperate. She'd even chosen the worst photo she had of herself: head so freshly shaved it gleamed, bottle in a brown bag, red-rimmed eyes. Mean eyes, as mean as she could make them. She remembered taking the photo. She'd just dropped Perry off and was ditching a car. From the front seat, snap, the photo was born. The green-and-blue blur behind her shoulder: a kid's car seat. Abandoned stuffed elephant, stiff with drool. It was because of that elephant she ditched the car only a block from where they'd taken it, and it was because of that elephant that she felt such meanness.

So she looked ugly and mean in the picture, but it had worked. Perry and some cousins were her only "friends" on the site. Until a couple weeks ago, when Baby Girl felt bored enough to go online and see that Jamey had friended her.

Hey there

Im new in town, lookin for freinds. U seem cool

Baby Girl felt embarrassed for him. The "Hey there," like he was some kind of grandpa. The typos. The "U." It all felt like he was trying to come off too casual, like her friendship meant more to him than he was willing to let on. His picture was of the back of his head— probably meant he was all fucked up in the face. She saw that Perry was friends with him, but Perry would let anyone be her friend on that site. Baby Girl wrote back:

You don't know shit bout shit, how you know if I'm cool?

Figured that would be that, better for him to find out that not everyone would just blindly accept him into their world. But within an hour he'd written back:

I like your hair

Did he really like her hair? Or was that his way of coming back at her? If he did like her hair, he might be someone worth knowing, someone who couldn't be fooled all that easily. And if it was his way of being sarcastic, Baby Girl almost liked him better for it. She wrote:

You're fuckin weird

Yeah I am, he'd responded. *Hope thats okay by u*

There'd be a message from him every time Baby Girl checked. It got to where she looked forward to going online and seeing what he'd say next. He asked for her number, something that no other boy had ever done, and Baby Girl gave it to him. He never called, just texted, always wanted to know where she was at, who she was with, what her and Perry were up to. Online one night he asked:

U ever ben with anyone?

Never mind, aint none of my bizness

But Baby Girl wanted to tell him. Wanted to say no, she'd never been with anyone, not all the way, didn't even let herself think about it too hard. She'd watched the way boys looked at Perry, had even sat on the other side of doors and, once, outside her own car, waiting for Perry to get done with a few of them. Had glanced over and seen Perry's leg, her toes flexing like she was trying to crack one of them, and that was a private horror to Baby Girl, worse, she felt strongly, than if she'd looked over and seen Perry naked, or moaning, or even stabbed. Wanted to say, *I don't even know if I'm attracted to you, you seem kind of simple and I haven't seen your face, but if you're asking me if I been with anyone so you can then ask me do I want to meet up and find out what it's all about, I will tell you yes, I'm begging you to let me say yes.*

But what she actually wrote was:

Haha, perv

What bout that freind your always with? he wrote. *U think shes slutty rite?*

Baby Girl's heart had been pounding, she was halfway at the computer and halfway already in the car, driving toward him, feeling terrified and disgusted and ready for whatever. Was he fat, was he missing teeth, would he see her in person and shut the door? But him asking after Perry had put Baby Girl back, all the way, in her chair.

Why you askin about her? she wrote.

LOL, just makin small talk, he responded.

She's no slut, watch what you say

I just thot I saw her around with a buncha differen guys, thats all

SO??? You a stalker? she wrote.

Then: *LOL*

Lately he'd been asking more about Perry, *U with your freind?* Shit, he probably had that pretyped and ready to send every time he didn't see Baby Girl online. At first she felt kind of flattered, like he was checking in on her to make sure she wasn't with no other boys, but now it felt like he wanted to know was she with Perry. They were having a conversation about music when he wrote,

Your freind like the same kinda music??

He knew her name, she'd written it and texted it to him a lot, but he always called Perry "your freind."

I know you're friends with her, why don't you just ask her yourself? she wrote.

Don't be like that Dayna. Baby Girl knew he'd say that, had almost wanted to type it herself so he could see how well she knew him. She'd told him her real name one night when they'd been chatting for hours, and her legs ached from sitting so long, and her wrists felt bruised from all the typing, and it seemed like they'd been talking about everything. He used her name only when he wanted her to know he was being serious. *Don't be like that Dayna.* But then:

Hey what r u wearing

LOL

He'd used her name, and then he'd laughed. She decided to give him what he was asking for.

I'm not wearing shit

I'm naked

It's cold in here so my nipples are hard

I have perfect nipples

I shave my pussy, you like that?

What are U wearing, motherfucker?

The word *pussy* blared from the screen. She had wanted to scare him. Baby Girl felt as cold and exposed as if she really was naked. *Jamey is typing.*

Whoa whoa

That aint what Im after

Your my freind

Im your freind rite?

Baby Girl didn't answer, just watched the cursor blink. Finally he said,

Talk to u later I guess
Jamey has signed off.

That was two nights ago. Nothing since. No texts, no online chatting. Baby Girl's yearning had felt as bright as a car alarm, a shrieking that filled her ears and flooded her body and scared the shit out of her. And for some reason, even though she wanted to talk about it with someone, it felt like something she should guard closely around Perry. Like if Perry knew she'd take it away and Baby Girl might walk up to the car one day to see the back of Jamey's head moving slow between Perry's legs, Perry's face bland as a tortilla, the *ping ping* of her toes cracking the only evidence that there was any life to her at all. So Baby Girl kept it to herself. She'd tell Perry when the time came, if the time came.

I have been online, she said now. *And didn't you get my text?*

Im just teasin, he said. *Ben thinkin bout u*

Baby Girl smiled again. *Been thinking about you too*

U out last nite?? he wrote.

Yeah . . . couldn't sleep so we went out thuggin, she wrote back.

With ur freind?

Baby Girl decided to let that one go, not get on his case about it, she was so glad to hear from him again.

Yeah she was there
I thot so
Im glad u aint disapeered

Me too, Baby Girl wrote, and she wanted to shout, to run in and tell . . . who? There wasn't no one.

I stil wana meetup u kno?

Me too, Baby Girl wrote again. So fucking tongue-tied by this no-faced stranger.

Alrite wel l lets talk l8r u got school

Okay I'll text you l8r, you fuckin dork. Something Baby Girl would never have typed normally. But it was cute, he was cute, he wanted to meet up with her. With *her.*

Lookin fwd

Jamey has signed off.

Baby Girl scrolled back up, reread their brief chat. *I stil wana meetup u know?* She felt like she could jump high as the roof. She felt . . . wanted. Attractive, even. Got up and threw her cereal bowl against the wall without even thinking why, just had to do something. Watched the sludge drip down in gory streams, puddle on the linoleum, her heart racing her lungs. She waited till she heard Charles turn the water off, then went over to clean up her mess. 'Cause one thing about Baby Girl she cherished was the thing that separated her from Charles, even before his accident: she could clean up her mess.

MYRA WOKE UP with a yolky taste in her mouth. She tried licking her lips but that only spread the yolk around, and the yolk dried fast. She was holding her glass from last night up against her heart and now she tipped it at her lips, but it was also dry. And then that carpet of regret started creeping up her body, moving rough and fast up her feet legs hips breasts neck head. Coating her in a raw rushing heat she did not welcome. Add to that how her stomach had nothing in it. That was going to be a problem.

She hadn't even *needed* the beer last night. Only drinking when a drink was needed was one of her rules. She had said this to Perry, and then Jim, many times over the years. *Don't worry. It's only when I need it.* She had just been bored, and a little disappointed. Most of the time the disappointment wasn't an issue. But then other times, like last night, with that boy, Pete, this young man interested in what she had to say, she'd find herself thinking of Jim and the flat plane of her life. How it was mostly defined now, no more surprises on the way, how Jim felt just fine with that, and her throat would close in like she'd swallowed a cherry pit and her throat didn't know was it better to swallow it down or cough it up.

Last night, before her first beer, she had come up behind Jim. Put her hands around his chest and rubbed his shirtfront. But he had already been dressed for work, and he didn't want to get undressed, then redressed. He'd turned and kissed her, as fast as a hummingbird's wing, on the lips. Didn't he know what that did to a woman?

Maybe that was why she'd let Pete sit awhile. It hadn't helped, though.

Had Perry come home? She hadn't heard her come home or leave for school. Which meant Jim hadn't come in to wake her when he got home, before driving Perry. Which meant Jim was annoyed with her, because she'd asked him to pour her a glass before he left. Well, it served him right.

She wished, sometimes, that Jim would get mad. But all he ever got worked up to was a mild kind of annoyance. She had once been pushed out of a moving car by a man angry with her, so most of the time Jim's mild, dulled reactions were just fine by her.

But they also added to the disappointment. They were small things that added up, like toothpicks in a Dixie cup, but still, they could stick you.

Shit. She had to get something in her stomach. She braced herself with her hand on the nightstand, knocking some bottles to the floor, but, a mercy, none broke. Still, the clattering sound ripped through her and instead of heading toward the kitchen, she headed for the bathroom. Knelt before the toilet. Heaved and spat.

When the heaving stopped, her knees singing with the pain, Myra got up, went into the kitchen to make some toast and coffee. Called Bill at the truck stop to apologize for not making her shift, explain that she was ill and couldn't come in.

"Mm-*hmm*," Bill said. "Well, we'll see you tomorrow, anyway." Myra knew he didn't believe her, but she was grateful for him playing along all the same.

She sat in the chair at the computer, dipped her toast into her coffee. Her neighbor had her music on, a constant cheerful braying that hammered Myra's skull. She must have bumped the mouse somehow because the computer screen suddenly flashed on. Perry's Facebook page was open. A boy named Jamey had called her beautiful. The picture he said it about was of Perry in a hat Jim had bought at the truck stop one day when he and Perry stopped by after school. The hat was as green as a leaf and there was a real golf tee balancing a real golf ball on the bill. Perry was smiling calmly, like it wasn't nothing more than a hair barrette. She could see why Perry had uploaded it. The green in the hat, the green in her eyes. She *was* beautiful. Too much eyeliner but that was a teenager's way. Myra swelled with pride.

She clicked on the boy's name. His page was empty, not much activity. A few days back he had liked a page about bass fishing. There was only a single photo of him and it was of the back of his head. He was facing a wide green field. His shoulders looked strong. He had seventeen Facebook friends. To Myra's knowledge, kids usually had "friends" in the thousands. Perry had more than two thousand herself. But then again, Perry was a girl. It seemed natural that a boy, a boy who liked bass fishing, wouldn't be as involved in some website. Myra guessed he joined just so he could get in touch with Perry. And that was sweet.

She closed the window, pushed herself away from the computer. Jim would be back from dropping Perry off soon. She'd have to look better than she did now. She didn't want him to think she was some kind of drunk, all her luster lost. She didn't want to be no toothpick in *his* Dixie cup.

DURING HOMEROOM the vice principal came on the intercom and announced that someone had set a fire out back of the Walmart, had melted a cart to uselessness, and there was tire track evidence so if anyone knew anything they'd better come forward. Perry wanted to laugh but everyone was listening real serious, even Ronny, who was the loudmouth in class and who did the kind of shit she and Baby Girl did nearly every weekend. Once, at a house party hosted by one of the junior girls, he called and ordered all the porn channels, just so he could watch them in the two hours he'd be there. Even *he* was listening politely, eyes cast down at his desk, acting like a serious crime had occurred.

Perry texted Baby Girl. *You hear that?? Fuckin classic.* It was like taking a temperature, holding the phone still, waiting for the vibration of her reply, waiting to see how bad the fever was.

Tire track evidence. That was the beauty of stealing cars. It wasn't their car, so even if they found the Mazda, it'd never be connected to them. They always wiped everything down. Last night they'd used wet wipes they'd found in the glove compartment.

Still no reply from Baby Girl. She could get like that, Perry knew. Real careful. She'd just take it up with her later. They needed to be on the same page. They needed to iron it all out.

"Students," Mrs. Gutherton said, "get out your homework. Or read a book. Do something so I don't have to get on you about doing something. Spend your time wisely."

Mrs. Gutherton had short curls that were always flattened in the back, and she wore turtlenecks every day, and her bra made her boobs look like two lumpy scoops of mashed potatoes, and she was never not *up to here* with her students. Being a teacher seemed like such an *oh well* kind of life.

Perry wanted her life to be purposeful. When she was a kid she thought becoming an adult meant you just found the right door and walked through it into a burst of light. Everything was easier through that door, because you'd found the answer.

Now that she was older, she knew it wasn't like that. She knew people sometimes came up to the door and kept walking right on past it. People like Baby Girl. Perry had narrowed it down to three doors. And *Teacher* sure as hell wasn't the name on any one of them.

"What, Ronny?" Mrs. Gutherton asked. He'd raised his hand, and now gripped the sides of his desk, bore down, released a long machine-gunning fart. A few boys laughed. The girl behind him threw a pencil at his head, ran for a seat three rows over. Sometimes school felt like a scene in a terrible sitcom, one that had a catch-phrase and at least two fart jokes per episode.

Mrs. Gutherton looked like she might be considering what Ronny did, like he'd asked a question or said something worth pondering. "Okay, Ronny," she said. "You may be dismissed. Give the princi-pal my regards." More sitcom talk. She patted at the back of her head. Just making it worse and worse. Perry had a pick comb in her purse, truly wanted to offer it up, but figured it would get her an in-vitation to the principal's office, too, or make the teacher think they could be friends.

"Man, it was just a joke," Ronny said. He was ignored. He shuf-fled out like his ankles were shackled.

That was another lesson Perry and Baby Girl had learned: Don't be caught off guard when the shit comes back on you. Expect that it will.

Baby Girl still hadn't replied. Perry passed the note she'd written over to Shanna, a girl with hair that looked pasted over her right eye, her left eye thickly lined in blue eyeliner. She was wearing a tight sparkly shirt like the kind Myra bought in bulk, back in the day. A momma-trying-to-be-sexy shirt. Shanna's tits looking more like pecs than anything. So many things to feel sorry over. In her note, Perry had written:

Hey—I saw on fbook that u know Jamey. What's his deal? He's clingy right??

After a minute, Shanna passed it back.

I mean, I know him from fbook. He friended me a while back but I haven't talked to him really all that much. He seemed nice tho. I like your top today!

Little hearts over every *i*. Smiley face at the end. Shanna was a real kiss-ass type, that one eye always wide and begging. Best not to stoke the flames by writing back and thanking her, especially since she didn't know anything anyway.

Later, in math class, the window a/c unit rattled on and off in five-minute intervals. Off just long enough so everyone started smelling, on long enough to dry the sweat. Perry liked the way her sweat smelled. Her own specific scent. Like sugar, and like butter left out for too long. Kind of sweet and kind of nasty. Baby Girl smelled like a sliced onion if she got too sweaty, but Perry had seen her caking her pits with Secret, had seen her spritzing that perfume you could get for $1.29 at the drugstore under her shirt, so it wasn't like Baby Girl wasn't trying. They had to sit alphabetically according to last names, so Baby Girl was behind Perry and at a diagonal, seated in the row all the way against the wall. She was still in the same clothes from the night before, but her hair fell in wet lines down her forehead, and Perry couldn't smell the onion yet, so it was clear she'd showered. Her lips outlined in brown and gleaming, like always. Perry looked at her, mouthed, *Why didn't you text me back?*

Why the fuck would I? she mouthed back, real slow and deliberate, like she was tough, like she had no idea how dumb she looked with a mouth drawn around her mouth. Still, if Baby Girl was really disturbed by something she'd have ignored Perry outright. So they were cool.

Bitch, Perry mouthed, turned around before Baby Girl could say anything back.

Travis usually sat in the row on the other side of Perry, but today his desk was empty.

It was nearly one o'clock. Perry felt cored, and the shell that was left ached. The classroom was as warm as a kitchen, Mr. Clark talking about tangents and cotangents in a nasally drone. Perry felt her lids pulling down, her eyes nearly closed when he'd say *tangent* or *cotangent* again, getting too rough with his *t*'s. Bringing her right back to the ache.

Travis walked in ten minutes before class was over. Perry checked his shoes. Silvery sneakers, like they were spun from webs. Mr. Clark watched Travis take his seat, holding his chalk in front of him, like it was important, leaving a ghost of dust across his middle. "All right," he said.

"Yeah," Travis said. "I apologize, Mr. Clark."

"All right," Mr. Clark said again.

Travis didn't have anything to write with, didn't even have his book or his green book bag. She had noticed this happening to him before, and now that Perry knew he worked all night long it made sense. It was hard for her to remember to bring everything after a night out with Baby Girl. She'd had to borrow pens and paper countless times from the boy in front of her, Matt, who she usually tried to copy off during quizzes. She nudged him now, pushing her fingertips into the flesh at his back. His T-shirt was hot and moist, stuck to him. He turned, smiling, ready to help, and Perry tried not to gawk at the gap between his front teeth. "Give Travis your other pen," she whispered. "And a piece of paper."

Matt looked from her to Travis. "Sure," he whispered, and quickly handed them over like Travis was mugging him. "But I need that pen back." He had never said that to Perry before. She probably had a dozen of his pens in her locker, on the floor of Baby Girl's car.

"Thanks," Travis whispered. "I'll make sure to give it back." He bowed his head, started writing down the scraps of equations Mr. Clark had written on the board throughout the class. Going through the motions was what he seemed to be doing.

He must have felt Perry watching him. Looked up at her with his big cow's eyes.

"You're welcome," she whispered. He nodded, and Perry was disappointed that he didn't smile at her. In her mind he had smiled, and she had smiled, and after class they'd walked together in the hall, out the front doors, into the woods . . . but there she stopped herself. She wouldn't be like that with him. And besides, he hadn't even smiled at her.

But he was probably as tired as Perry was, more even, since he'd been working all night. Mopping and cooking and whatever else. Helping that old witch waitress adjust her wig just so. *Pam.* Again Perry found herself thinking how nice it'd be to go back to the trailer and have Myra and Jim be gone, lay down on her bed with Travis. Take a nap, nothing else.

Perry's phone vibrated. A text from Baby Girl. *Pay attention bitch! need 2 copy ur homework l8r!!*

She clicked her pen, ready to take notes. It occurred to her that she wanted, very badly, for Travis to think she was smart.

IT WAS A THIRTY-MINUTE DRIVE to and back from the high school, so when Jim got home Myra had managed to shower and get into a clean dress; the white one with the tiny blue flowers dotted everywhere. Made Myra feel younger. Cleaner. The beery sheets she'd thrown into the small closet washing machine were frothed and rinsed, ready for the dryer, though Myra knew they'd have a better chance hung from a line, old as the dryer was. But that seemed like a lot today. Too much.

"Hey," Jim said to her, standing at the front of the hallway, hands on his hips. "You eat?"

"Surely did," she answered. They were out of fabric softener; they were always out of something. "Can I make you a bite?"

"Might make myself some eggs," Jim said. Myra was no cook. Still, she wanted Jim to see that she'd offered. She followed him into the kitchen, sat at the tiny nook table to watch him. He cracked some eggs into Perry's old plastic bowl. A chipped cartoon fish with a mouth full of teeth grinned from the bowl's center.

"Myra," Jim started to say, whipping the eggs with a fork. She loved the sound of her name when he said it. So serious. Like she was someone worth knowing.

"Mmm?" she asked. She felt lulled by the sound of the fork, tiny pings and the liquid swish of the eggs. "What is it?"

"I am pretty sure Perry was out all night last night," Jim said, turning his back to her to pour the eggs into the pan. He was testing the waters, seeing how Myra would react. Because she knew she had done wrong last night, she gave him a taste of what he wanted.

"You're kidding," she said, working a thread of shock into her voice. "Again? And after all the talks you've had with her."

It wasn't that Myra didn't worry for her child. She did. Only not for stuff like staying out all night. Instead, Myra worried Perry wouldn't appreciate her youth, her beauty, all the chances she was being given to create moments she could hold on to. To make her life a jewelry box full of shiny things rather than a cabinet that rarely got dusted.

But Myra had gone too far. Or maybe she hadn't gone far enough. Her words, instead of coming out sincere, had landed flat and unfeeling. She sat up straighter. She needed to pay better attention.

"Anyway," Jim said, his back still turned. "She was in one piece and she went to school. So maybe I'm wrong and she *was* home after all."

"I'm glad we have you to worry after us," she said. "Jim," she said, when he still hadn't turned. When he did a moment later she shook some pepper into her hand, held it out to him.

"No thanks," he said. His eyes held her face a beat too long; he was watching her, waiting to see if she knew Perry had been out. She couldn't let on that she knew, couldn't let him know a strange boy had been in the trailer drinking with her while her daughter was out in the night with that half-bald girl. Myra hated that she felt like she had to pretend in front of her husband.

Finally he turned back, raked a spatula through his eggs. "You sleep okay?" His way of dropping the subject. Myra felt tired. She knew Jim was tired. Perry was tired. They were on a carousel that wouldn't stop.

"I might go over there and knock on her door," Jim was saying. He meant the neighbor, the polka music. "I know she's old and she enjoys it but we all need our sleep." He was already halfway out the screen door; he closed it gently behind him.

Myra went to the bathroom, wet her hands, flicked water onto her face with her fingertips. The carpet of regret had returned, her face was as hot as a stone in the sun. She heard Jim knocking on the neighbor's door, calling *Mrs. Kozlowski? Mrs. Kozlowski?* The music stopped. Jim and the neighbor murmured to each other. Myra looked into her own face in the mirror. Where Perry's looks had come from, she didn't know. She herself was blond and blue-eyed, and Perry's father was Italian. Myra was pretty sure about that, anyway. It hadn't been a long courtship.

But sometimes she saw Perry catching her own reflection in a window, that quick appraisal, and Myra could see how Perry was pleased with what she saw. *That* was what she had given to Perry.

She heard Jim come back in, remove the pan from the stove. The neighbor's music started up again, turned down a smidge.

"Jim," Myra called. "Come here for a sec." She appraised herself in the mirror, straightened her neck and shoulders, allowed that flood of knowing vanity to fill her face. She had held the attention of a young man for quite some time the night before. When Jim appeared in the doorway, she took him by his belt and led him into the bedroom.

IF YOU LET YOUR EYES LOSE FOCUS everything becomes a smear. That's how Baby Girl liked to get through class. The teacher a moving smear of brown and gray, his voice like someone was rubbing an eraser over it: the words were there but you had to work hard to find them.

She used to be good at this shit. Math, English. School. Back when it felt like it mattered, paying attention and doing homework and playing the clarinet and never missing class, not even when she was sick, not even when Charles called collect from jail at five in the morning.

She checked her phone. No new texts. That was all right, she told herself. That was fine, they'd talk *18r*.

"Dayna," the teacher said. "What'd I say about the next time you bring your phone to class?"

She let her eyes focus. Even still, Mr. Clark looked like a smear. She hadn't had the time to fully convince herself that no new texts was actually just fine, and maybe that's why she answered, "That you'll set it to vibrate and put it up your butt?"

A boy in the back of the room exploded with laughter. Some other kids giggled behind their hands. Baby Girl hated them for it. They should think she was an asshole. What she said wasn't even all that clever, had come out before she had time to stop it. Perry hadn't laughed, either. That was happening more and more these days.

She began packing up her things. She knew she'd be sent to the principal's office, and she wanted to make it as easy on Mr. Clark as possible, the least she could do. She also knew she'd walk right past the office, push out the doors, run to her car to wait for Perry. She could feel the hard slaps her feet would make, could feel the heat of the treeless parking lot. Was already composing a new text to him: *What u doin?* or even just *Hey*.

"Nope," Mr. Clark said. "You're staying right here in this classroom. And you're coming up here to finish the equation we've started as a class."

He held out the chalk. Baby Girl felt excited, she couldn't help it. Back in the day she loved to write on the board, loved erasing what she'd written and writing it all over again, only neater. Loved to have the class watch her get an answer right, please the teacher, be the best.

But now she felt embarrassed by her excitement. She dropped her bag as hard as she could on the floor, walked up and snatched the chalk from the teacher's hand. The equation had three different letters in it, or was one of the letters a multiplication sign? She felt ashamed that she didn't know, angry that Mr. Clark knew she didn't know and was making an example of her.

Sometimes when it felt like there was no way out Baby Girl could feel her body getting cold, like it was shutting down so she could think. Like the time a man in his boxers had held up a bat and swung it at her and Perry, yelling how he was going to call the cops. At first it was like Baby Girl was hearing and seeing everything all at once, the man yelling, Perry laughing, a car going by two streets over. And then she had gone cold, could see the way out as if it had been blasted with a flashlight: scream, charge at the man, yank down his boxers, run.

And now here she was again, cold as a lizard. The equation ordered itself, she knew the answer was *26x*. Wrote it on the board, wrote *suck* and *dicks* around it, so the answer read, "Suck 26x dicks."

Mr. Clark looked like his boxers had landed around his ankles. The boy in the back exploded again. Baby Girl threw the chalk at him on her way out. She hated him, she felt sorry for Mr. Clark and that made her hate him, hate herself.

Heat, footslaps, the wham of her car door. She hunched low, breathing the thick hot air in the car. The bell rang; the bell rang again. Perry would be in biology now. She sent two texts: *P, I'm in the car* and *Hey what u doin?* Added a smiley face, because it seemed more girly, less desperate for a response, but at the last second Baby Girl decided it made her seem high or dense. She fucked up the deletion, though, so her text read:

Hey what u doin? :

No smile, just eyes, like Baby Girl wanted him to know she wasn't playing, she was looking for him, she wasn't even blinking, she was looking so hard.

He probably wouldn't even notice the eyes. She hoped he wouldn't, she hoped he would.

THEY WERE WATCHING A VIDEO about predatory animals when she got Baby Girl's text. She could have stayed and watched that video, it was pretty interesting, especially since she was the only girl who didn't hide her eyes when the animals would catch something, bite deep into flesh, the zebra or whatever thrashing and then woops, there's its ribs. Perry wasn't coldhearted. She just wasn't scared like the other girls.

She could have stayed and felt just fine with that, but she didn't want to miss out on a ride from Baby Girl, didn't want to miss out on the feeling of driving out of the parking lot while everyone else was still stuck inside the school. She asked to go to the bathroom, threw the hall pass in the garbage on her way out, waited for the parking lot guard to chug around the bend, out of sight. The school was a flat brown building with a parking lot in front and a bunch of trailers parked in what used to be the football field out back. The school had expanded enough to need trailer classrooms, and it didn't have enough money to keep up with a football team, so problem solved. The parking lot guard patrolled the parking lot and the trailers, so kids always waited for the golf cart to make its way over toward the old football field before they made a run for it. Perry never ran, though. Running made you look guilty.

Baby Girl was hunched low in the driver's seat, staring at her phone. Perry got in and Baby Girl backed out of the parking spot, drove them through the gates, sped through the yellow light at the corner, still hunched. Perry felt it, she felt that freedom she'd been expecting, the sun suddenly brighter and the air quieter and the grass so green it hurt her eyes, everything seeming to say that what she'd done was right.

They were on the other side, they were out, and the possibilities lay before them like dashes on a highway. Some days they never found a reason to be out, and maybe today was like that. And it wasn't like they were trying all that hard. Baby Girl drove lazily, full stops at corners even when there wasn't a stop sign, checking her phone again and again like she was waiting on something to come through.

Perry's own phone vibrated. A text from Jamey. *U with your freind? U gonna get online? I wanna talk 2 u.*

Later, she wrote back. She didn't want to talk to him, maybe ever again. *Oooh baby.* Thinking of Travis typing those words, now that was something to consider.

They drove around, parked at the McDonald's. Perry wondered if it was the same shift as when she and Jim had gone through that morning, if the girl with the lazy eye and long green nails would hand them their burgers if they hit the drive-through. Baby Girl looked at her phone again. "Who you waiting on?" Perry asked.

"Charles," she said. "He's supposed to text me when he's ready to get picked up."

Perry knew that was a lie. Charles didn't text and Baby Girl picked him up every day at the same time. "Mm-hmm," Perry said. A fat man walked into the McDonald's, antlers of sweat on his shirt, spreading out from his spine. Perry liked to ask herself would she go for different kinds of men: fat, ugly, old. But no, not today. Today all she could think of was Travis, how he hadn't smiled back at her, how when he'd handed the pen back at the end of class, he'd smiled at Matt.

Baby Girl's phone tittered. Perry snatched it out of her hand, scraping Baby Girl's wrist with her nails, holding her off with her other hand so she could read.

U with your freind?

Jamey's number. Baby Girl mashed Perry's face with her hand until Perry could taste the salt on her fingers. She dropped the phone and it clattered over the gearshift, fell between the seats.

Perry's face felt hot, branded where Baby Girl's hand had been. "Don't," Baby Girl said. The heat traveled, covered Perry's whole body. "Fuck you," Perry said.

Sometimes Perry wondered how they were friends, or even if *friends* was the word for what they were. They never talked about boys, Perry had never asked Baby Girl if she'd even touched a wiener before. They didn't talk, really, they just did. Perry'd had a crush on Charles a long time ago, before his accident, before she filled out the training bra Myra had gotten on sale at Walmart. Perry wrote him a note saying how she felt. The next day Baby Girl brought it back to her. "I read this," she said. "I took it before Charles could see it. You don't want him seeing it." Perry thought she was saving her from embarrassment, that Baby Girl knew Charles would laugh and keep ignoring her, but then she said, "You don't want him liking you." Perry never asked her why, too embarrassed that she didn't already know.

And that's probably why she didn't tell Baby Girl what she knew. That Jamey was also texting her. The text just before the one Perry saw on Baby Girl's phone said, *I wanna meet up with u and your freind*. He was only texting her to get to Perry.

Baby Girl got out of the car, went into the McDonald's. She knew she wasn't supposed to follow. Perry could see her inside, typing into her phone. She should have stayed to see what happened to that zebra.

When Baby Girl dropped Perry home, Myra's and Jim's cars were there, but their bedroom door was closed. Myra probably with a pillow over her head to block the light and Jim probably still in his work pants. He had another shift that night.

Perry got online. Her chat was already blinking, just like she knew it would be.

Hey girlie, missed u

She typed fast, couldn't wait to bust him. *Why you messin with my friend? I saw your text to her*

He didn't answer right away. *Jamey is typing.* Perry got up for a ginger ale, came back to see that he'd finally spit it out.

U jealous?? :p

You checkin up on me?

Aw girlie I'm just innerested in your life, he wrote.

Then: *We cant have the same freinds??*

It's spelled friends. And why you so interested in my life? Perry signed off before he could answer. Her face still felt hot, and she didn't care what his answer was, only that he knew she knew.

MYRA HAD TAKEN HIM by the belt, had led him to their bed. He knew men, other guards, who were just grateful their wives could cook, who confiscated magazines from prisoners and saved them for their breaks, going at themselves in a locked stall, emerging sweaty and red-faced and pretending it was just a difficult dump. He had never had to be one of those men, Myra had always taken care of him in that regard. He was grateful for that, but he was envious of the other men, too. Such cheerful wives. Sandwiches and cookies in Ziplocs, no foamy glasses to clean up at home.

But he'd rather make his own lunch, he supposed, than be a man in a stall.

Phil was at the front desk. "Morning," he said as Jim walked up. Phil greeted him the same at the start of every night shift, and Jim appreciated it. Made him feel almost normal.

"Morning," Jim answered, and pushed through the first set of doors. With every door he pushed through, the light changed. Like they used the good bulbs up front and the harsh fluorescents farther in. He didn't know why anyone bothered pretending prison offered any kind of rehabilitation; even if the food didn't come powdered or in cans or already ruined, the light was enough to drive any man to violence—an unnatural bluish white light that hummed like a bee under your pillow. And they never turned the lights off. No telling what a man could do with a few seconds and a dark corner. Can't take that chance. If a light blew out, it was immediate lockdown until it was repaired. The men were just too bored not to be creative.

Ten hours of that light left Jim feeling like an animal. And he got to leave it after that. These men had to stay. Once, a meek, whip-thin drug addict on a three-year stint had come in, and it was clear he had meant to stay under the radar, never asking for seconds, never looking anyone in the eye. Jim had hope for him, had even stopped outside his cell to talk about the weather. The addict talked about feeling the warm rain on his face once he got out. But those lights. After a month the man had to be thrown in solitary for writing *CRACK* in his own fecal matter on his roommate's bed.

Jim rounded the corner and saw that O'Toole was also waiting to be buzzed in to the next area. "Morning," Jim said.

O'Toole snapped his fingers what felt like mere centimeters from Jim's nose. "Get a cup of coffee, Tipton. It ain't fucking morning." Jim grabbed O'Toole's hand so tight he could hear the surprise *pop pop* of O'Toole's knuckles cracking. Happened almost before he could stop himself. Like he had turned the channel and now he was watching some new scene. O'Toole wasn't a big man, but he'd fight back if it was called for, and the thought made Jim let go.

"What the fuck, Tipton?" O'Toole was panting, his breath warm and moist.

"Just kidding around," Jim said. He could barely get the words out. Lactic acid was pouring into his muscles. He felt feverish, and sorry, and filled with dread. "Go on ahead," he told O'Toole, though the man had already turned.

Sometimes Jim thought if he could just take Perry to work, if she could just see what breaking the rules did to a person . . . but then this shit with O'Toole reminded him that life wasn't no better on the other side of the bars. He shook his head. Had to stop thinking like that. But it was true. Taking Perry to work would only show her that you're damned if you do and goddamned if you don't.

Jim waited at one door for a buzz, crossed through it, waited at another door for a buzz, crossed through that. The buzzing echoed behind him in a long, retreating wail.

Two hours into his shift, five minutes before Jim could take his break, he heard the muffled sounds of a quiet jump in one of the cells. It was the middle of the night, but that was when inmates were the most keyed up, too much silence, too much time to think. Men never screamed or called for help when they were being jumped; that was part of the code. At first he couldn't tell if it was on the second tier, where he was when he heard it, or below him, or even if it was on the side he was supposed to be patrolling, but he could hear it clear as day: the unmistakable sound of fists and feet and elbows landing in the soft meat of a body, which meant the owner of the body had stopped fighting back.

He couldn't see O'Toole anywhere, so he shouted the man's name. "I got it," O'Toole answered from the far corner, where three other guards were pushing into a cell on O'Toole's side. The guards and O'Toole started shouting for the men to get down, hands behind their heads, their voices guttural and angry, like rage had taken form and was all mouth.

Some of the inmates on Jim's side were getting loud, yelling across about what they could and couldn't see. One of the guards pulled the downed man out by his arms. A blood bib on his sweatshirt, his face all smear. The inmates who could see cheered, the ones who couldn't yelled, *Who down? He dead?* The rage was taking Jim now. Men cheering at the pulped man. He felt his nightstick in his hand, suddenly, and he beat the railing with it until his ears rang.

Later, as they were clocking out together, Jim asked O'Toole what the fight was about. "Deck of playing cards," was his answer. O'Toole wasn't looking Jim in the face, still frosty over the scuffle they'd had clocking in, and he walked quickly to get ahead of Jim and out to the parking lot. Jim slowed, his legs tired, his whole self tired. He didn't want to get in that truck and drive home, and he didn't want to turn around and work another shift. He stood in the parking lot, the sky the pale blue and yellow of a child's room, the day already warm. O'Toole drove by, didn't return Jim's wave. He knew he could have punched O'Toole till his brain was bent if he'd felt just a bit more provoked than he had. It occurred to Jim that it was in a man's nature to fight, to wound. Playing cards sold for a dollar in the commissary. A single dollar.

THE DENNY'S WAS A SHORT WALK from the trailer, just up one exit. Stay close to the guardrail and try not to look directly at the headlights coming fast, get off at the next exit.

She wanted to see Travis, so she went to see him. *Easy as pie*, as Myra would say.

It felt strange not to call and ask Baby Girl to drive her. But then again, what did she need Baby Girl for? In the past she'd used Baby Girl's car to get closer to a boy, but she didn't even know what she wanted to do with Travis yet. And he didn't seem like the type to rush to the backseat anyway.

And plus her face burned every time she thought of Baby Girl's hand on her cheek, mashing her lips into her teeth. She knew Baby Girl was capable of shit like that, of course she knew. But she'd never had to deal with it coming back at her. If it happened again . . . if it happened again, what?

Anyway, she told herself.

The Denny's smelled like syrup and bacon and bleach. The same waitress, Pam, moving from table to table. Perry sat at the counter.

"What you got a taste for, hon?" Pam asked. It didn't seem like she remembered Perry. It was likely people came in at all hours and gave her shit, their faces all blurred together, a tapestry of assholes. Perry felt grateful that she could drop her guard.

"Coffee," she said.

"Mm-hmm, and?"

"And that's it," Perry said.

"You still got to tip at least fifteen percent," Pam told her. "Sometimes you young kids don't seem to know that." She put a cup and saucer in front of Perry, poured coffee into the cup so quick that it sloshed over the side. "Cream and sugar right there," she said, pointing.

Perry knew the thug code meant she should say something back, something that'd stop Pam in her tracks, something that might even get herself tossed out, but it felt like a lot, coming up with the right thing to say and then delivering it with just enough acid. Without Baby Girl there, it didn't seem worth it.

"Whatever," she said, but the waitress was already at the other end of the counter, helping an old man choose between waffles and pancakes. Perry decided now was the time, got up and walked around the counter and through the metal double doors into the kitchen.

Travis was leaning up against the sink, holding his math book with both hands, staring at it like he was watching a horror movie play out. A fat man with white hair trapped under a hairnet was at the stove moving eggs around. "Hey," he said, pointing his spatula at Perry. "This is definitely not the ladies' room. You ain't supposed to be back here."

Travis looked up. At first it was like he didn't recognize her, but then he closed his book and walked quickly over. "Hey," he said. "You really shouldn't be back here."

"I know," Perry said. "I wanted to see you."

Travis looked back at the man in the hairnet, now with his hands on his hips, the spatula held tight at his waist. His apron looked diseased, pocked with brown flecks. "I'll walk you out," Travis said. He held one of the metal doors open, waiting for her to follow. She followed him back through the dining room—Pam helping a couple with a baby now—and out through the front doors. She tried to check her reflection in the glass of one of those claw vending machines, but he was holding the door, watching.

In the parking lot they stood facing each other, he in the circle of light from one of the old-timey streetlamps and Perry in the dark just outside of it.

"What are you saving money for?" Perry asked. Her voice felt muffled by the traffic, the endless hum of the traffic and the lights and her own heart in her ears.

"Huh?"

"The first time I saw you here you said you were saving money."

"Oh," Travis said, and was quiet, considering his answer. "Actually, my mom lost her job, and all she could get was part-time work, so I got this job to help out."

Myra had never asked Perry to get a job. Jim had mentioned it once or twice but more as a way for Perry to grow up a little, not because they needed the money. She felt sorry for Travis, but not in the same way she felt sorry for Matt, with his plump, sweaty back and his eager eyes and his cheeks full of zits. She felt sorry that Travis had to do shit he didn't want to do, that his back was against the wall. She wanted more than ever to put her hands on him, make him feel like something was worth it.

"Did you hear what I said, earlier?" Perry asked him.

"You said you wanted to see me," he said.

"Oh."

"For what?"

Perry wasn't prepared for that. Usually if you told a boy you wanted to see him the rest just fell into place, like dominoes. Just had to tip that one piece, no more effort than the flick of a finger.

So instead of answering, Perry asked him, "Are you bad at math?"

"What? I don't know, it ain't my best subject, I guess." He edged aside, out of the light.

"Me, too."

In the dark his face seemed kinder. Perry wondered what he

thought of her face, if he thought of her face. "You think I'm pretty?" she asked.

"Of course," he said, quickly. He took a step back, to get into the light, but he only made it halfway. He'd definitely thought of her face.

"Good," she told him. She walked forward, fast, so he wouldn't have the chance to get away. Kissed him, or tried to, her lips landing on the side of his mouth. She kept her face close to his. He smelled like bleach, and like he'd had a soda not too long prior. She wasn't looking to start something with him, right there in the parking lot, she now saw that as clear as crystal. But what was it, then? She couldn't straighten it out, just knew she wanted to be near him.

"Thank you for saying I'm pretty," she whispered. She hoped her breath was all right, wished she carried gum or mints with her like Baby Girl always did.

"You know you are," he said. He put his hands on her shoulders, and for a second Perry almost thanked him for that, too, here it was, here was the giving in. But instead of drawing her nearer he pushed off, backed up. "I got to get back inside," he said. "Nice seeing you." He jogged backward, turned when he got to the door. Perry watched him, his white shirt and black pants against all that yellow light, until he rounded the corner to the kitchen and was gone.

Two men in paint-splattered coveralls came out of the Denny's, the taller man picking his teeth. Perry guessed theirs was the green truck in the parking lot. The highway sounded like rain when it came down hard on the roof of the trailer. So many cars. The thought of walking back seemed like an eternity Perry didn't have to spend. She leaned up against the truck. They'd surely give her a ride, she wouldn't even have to ask. She hated asking.

PERRY IS SIGNED OFF.

Jamey hoped it was a mistake, Perry being unavailable to him for so long, hoped her Internet had just fritzed. He checked and he checked again. Still no Perry. He knew it was Dayna's fault, knew she couldn't keep those big nasty lips closed.

His momma lolled, he could see the rumpled white flesh at the tops of her thighs. He felt like *Fuck her*, only which her he meant he wasn't sure. Both. His momma would be waking soon, and damned if he could find it in himself to be there to answer when she asked did she look pretty, not for a momma but for a woman. He couldn't say, *Of course, Momma*, not one more time. He texted Dayna, *Why u letting your freinds read ur texts?* because fuck her, he let the door slam behind him on his way out because fuck her, he walked over to Perry's trailer because fuck her, fuck her, fuck her.

Her momma was drinking a beer, flicking from site to site on the computer. Her sandal dangled from her toe. Jamey could tell she had once been a beautiful woman, the delicate way she rolled her ankle, the way she held her back so straight and sure. He might have turned his attentions to her if she'd been younger. Now her skin, though pale and without the veins that inched along his own momma's legs like the legs of some insect, looked worked over. Like dough that hadn't been kneaded, like her flesh might lose its hold, become a pile. Perry was perfect. The right age, the right look, so beautiful and mean. Jamey wanted to hold it in his hands, whatever it was.

Sometimes he wanted to crush it in his hands. That couldn't be helped.

And there was Perry's picture. Myra was on her Facebook page. She scrolled a bit. Perry always had tons of new shit on her wall. If Myra looked at his Facebook page there wouldn't be nothing to see. Other people had new stuff happening all the time, new photos at least, but that was too dangerous for him. The only good photo of himself he had was the one he used, and it was of the back of his head. Choosing that photo felt like a sign of good luck now, something he finally did right.

Jamey felt a tightening in his pants. He got like that whenever he felt nervous or scared. He nearly put his hand down there, merely as a comfort, a protective shell, and then suddenly Myra closed the page, spun in her chair like she was just admiring the view of the living room. It didn't make sense until Jim came into view, shirtless, his hair sticking up. Jamey had never seen Jim looking unkempt. It came as a shock, this man Jamey had seen every day for years, this man Jamey had felt sure was made of engine parts and cogs and second hands on the inside, this man everyone would tell you was one of the good ones right up until you felt a sting across the back of your knees. Jamey opened his mouth wide, for what he wasn't sure. To laugh? Shout? He ended up gulping air like a drowned man surfacing, backing away from the window, rounding the corner and running back to his momma's trailer.

Only that was a dead end, too. Not welcome at one place, not willing to go in at the other. He guessed that's what porch steps were for. Sat down and relaxed for one full second before he realized he'd shown Dayna his hand. As if on cue, a text came in: *How tha fuck you know bout that?* He didn't know why Perry was friends with this girl. This half-bald thing. First thing to go, once everything worked out.

Jamey pocketed his phone. He'd go on patrol tonight, only he'd stay out of sight this time. The gun was just a conversation starter, that was all. And it had already worked on Perry's momma. Still, it was loaded. Never know when a good BB might come in handy.

He bet Perry tasted like strawberry lip gloss. Pineapple would be his second choice. He took his gun and stood in the shadows between the two trailers again, waiting for her.

THEY DIDN'T EVEN MAKE PERRY sit in the middle seat. One got in the driver's side and one got in the passenger's side, slid into the middle. She'd been expecting the middle seat, had been prepared to hold her legs just so, didn't want to be touching either man's thigh.

But here she was in the passenger seat, more than enough space on either side of her, neither man making any moves. It was a relief, and it was a disappointment.

She'd been hoping Travis would come out to mop the floors or bus a table right as she was getting into the truck. Maybe he'd get angry, maybe he'd run out and pull her out of there. But he'd never appeared anyway.

Now she was just grateful it was a short ride to her home, not long enough to learn anything about these men, definitely not long enough for them to try anything with her.

"You work there or something?" the driver asked. His voice had a slight accent to it.

"No," Perry said. "I was just there for some coffee."

"Oh," he said. "'Cause we saw you talking to that boy in the parking lot. He your boyfriend?"

The man in the middle seat turned to face her, listening.

"No," Perry said, thinking how Travis had touched her only to push her away. "He's just someone I go to school with."

Her exit came into view, the green sign growing larger. For a second Perry wondered if the man would truly pull off, or if he'd keep driving, speeding her toward some storage locker or closet dungeon. She put her fingers through the door handle, ready to jump out if she needed to.

But the man put on his signal, slowed, pulled off.

"I like their pancakes," Middle Seat said. "I like to crumble my bacon over them. Jorge likes their grand ham."

"Grand *slam*," the driver said. They both laughed. Perry flooded with relief to see the sign leading into the trailer park. Neither man had said anything about how she looked, didn't even say *If I was your age*, not even a low whistle. They were just grown men giving a child a ride home. Perry felt mildly disgusted.

"You can drop me here," she said. "Mine's the one just over there, and it'll be hard for you to back your truck out once you pull in there."

The driver put the truck into park. "Okay then," he said. "You be good."

"Yeah, be good," Middle Seat said. He put his arm around Perry's shoulders, like he was her uncle giving her a hug.

Something pinged off the windshield just then, making a small spider crack in the middle.

"What in heck?" the driver said. He gripped the wheel, hunched, eyes wild to see what it was.

"Sometimes kids throw rocks," Perry said. It was true—Perry had thrown rocks herself, as a child. Never hard enough to crack a windshield, but she wanted to say something to soothe the men, to make them leave.

"This is the company truck," the man said. His voice cracked on the word *company*.

"I'm real sorry," Perry said, opening her door. "Real sorry." She turned and ran for the trailer, didn't stop running until she was inside with the door closed. She could hear the truck idling, the men likely deciding whether to get out and find whoever threw the rock, but then she heard it backing out, driving off.

That was the right decision, she thought to herself. Knowing who threw the rock wouldn't make the crack go away. But who had thrown it? There weren't many kids in the park these days. Whoever it was, they were lucky. Those men had shovels in the bed of that truck, and it could have got ugly.

The trailer felt moist. Her momma had run a bath, was probably half asleep in there by now.

She switched on the TV. Ten o'clock news on every channel. Why had Travis been so rushed to get back inside? Maybe it had been her breath. Maybe she'd missed something—he had a girl-friend, or he was a gentleman. But she knew she hadn't.

She heard footsteps, moving from a walk to a run, heading away from the trailer. Whoever it was didn't have far to go, she could hear the footsteps all the way until they stopped, could hear them climb-ing the metal steps to a trailer. Neighborhood kid, probably the one with the rock. She went to the window, yelled from the screen. "Hey, don't be throwing no rocks!" A door slammed, she knew she'd been heard.

"What?" her momma called. Her voice sounded thick with sleep and probably beer. What did she have to do to get Travis to . . . what? Touch her? The thought made her long for the dark of her bedroom, where she could think it some more.

"Nothing," she called back.

She switched the light on in her room, then switched it off again. Her body was tired but her mind was racing. Even if she wanted to, she couldn't call Baby Girl. Give the bitch her space. She could get online, talk to Jamey, who'd surely be on waiting for her. But that seemed like a lot. He'd want to know why she'd signed off, he'd want to keep saying *Oooh baby* to her. Instead she lay on her bed, trying not to think how the night stretched before her like an unlit highway.

THE PRISONERS GOT QUIET now when they saw him drawing near. A few had seen him beat the railing with his nightstick, knew he'd jabbed Herman in the eye. They'd heard the man scream, and word had traveled via whispers and signals and whatever else these prisoners had devised to communicate with each other that Tipton wasn't in no mood. Even Carver, the other walker, left Jim alone. Some shifts they'd call across to each other, "You seen the game?" or "Weekend plans?" But not tonight. Jim was glad for a quiet night, they were few and far between, but he was also resentful of it, being treated like a loose case this way. It seemed like everywhere he went someone was watching for his reaction. Myra watching for him to notice the beer glass. Perry watching for him to notice liquor on her breath, the bags under her eyes. The prisoners watching to see what mood he was in, the other guards watching for the same. All of them making that knot in his back grow, pulse, that other heart lodged in his back thumping wave after wave of disappointment. They were all disappointments. He nearly laughed out loud. Not one of them living up to any kind of potential. Potential what? Was he living up to his potential? He wanted to laugh again, the kind of laugh he'd experienced as a boy when he fell from a tree onto his back. A laugh that quickly turned to loud babyish sobs, aimed right up into the sky. Myra should drink, Perry should sneak out at night, he should beat prisoners when the mood struck.

He allowed himself a smile, but only a smile. He wasn't a boy anymore. He was an adult, he had to find reasons not to lie on the ground and wail. On his break he'd get a fresh cup of coffee. It was only two hours until he could punch out. Nasty men like Herman were locked up where he could see them, not out prowling around on the lookout for ain't-nobody-can-get-me-type girls. Girls like Perry. Girls who just seemed to be asking for it. But that wasn't a fair thought, either. Who goes around asking to be messed with?

PERRY MADE FUN OF IT, and it was clear she felt a little embarrassed, but Baby Girl had always liked the trailer park where Perry lived. Most people kept their shit real neat, little potted plants and sets of chimes and even a birdbath out in front of one. There wasn't hardly any trash in the yards, no rusted-up cars on cinder blocks, no smudge-faced kids in bloated diapers running wild. And the closeness of the trailers to each other made it feel all cozy, like a bunch of people got together and decided to live within arm's reach of each other. At night you could hear what was on people's televisions, what they argued about, and once Baby Girl had heard a woman praying.

Of course, there were a few trailers in the park that you wanted to avoid, trailers with music and yelling and shit flying from the windows, trailers with dogs on chains or bags of trash rotting out front. Trailers with people that didn't know no better, or didn't care to. Best just to look past, to the people that did.

Still, Baby Girl liked the trailer park because it was different from where she lived, which was a neighborhood full of gray and brown houses and people polite to your face. All fences and cul de sacs and garages. The trailer park didn't have none of that, it was more real. Easier to be a girl with a half-shaved head who didn't give a *fuck*, you was just one of many different kinds in the trailer park.

It was such a sorry thing, being in some weird girl fight with Perry. She and Perry should be beyond normal girl stuff, Baby Girl felt convinced. Especially when it was about some dumb motherfucker using one to get to the other, as she now knew Jamey was doing. *Fuck him*, she told herself for the millionth time. Couldn't get the hope that he'd give up on Perry and try with her out of her mind, though. No matter how many *fuck him*s she chanted. And this made her hate him even more.

It had been days since they'd talked. A whole weekend had passed. Then Perry had texted *Quit acting like a little bitch* the night before, and that was why this morning Baby Girl had driven over, parked in front of the trailer. Perry calling her a bitch meant things were getting back to normal.

A car honked, Jim driving up behind her. She'd have to back up, around his truck, to let him in. Instead, he put the truck in park, got out, came around to her window. "You driving Perry to school to-day?" he asked her, leaning in. His collar was a faint yellow. Charles got ring around the collar too.

"Yeah," she said. "I thought I might."

"Just make sure you end up at school," he said. "Don't get side-tracked." His voice was quiet, like it was only a suggestion; it was clear he was trying not to sound too harsh.

Baby Girl liked Jim. He tried real hard to keep it all together. She might've just said, *Sure, of course, we're going to school, you bet.* Instead she said, "You should sprinkle some baking soda in the wash. You got ring around the collar."

Jim straightened, backed away. A strong breeze caught in his hair. The neighbor's chimes went ape shit. He ran his hand over his face like he was trying to smooth down the wrinkles. "Yeah," he said, "I know I do."

At last Perry emerged. Waved a Pop-Tart in the air like a stolen wallet, all *Look what I got.*

"We're going to school," Baby Girl said, but it wasn't clear if Jim heard. Perry got in, didn't offer the Pop-Tart. As they backed up she said, "Are we really, though?"

JAMEY STOOD in his hiding spot, watched them pull out. Perry licked her fingers, that friend of hers bobbing her head, the loud, thumping beat hitting him in his sinuses, then fading as they drove off. When he was a teenager he hated school, never hardly went, but now he felt envious that they had somewhere to go, somewhere they were expected. In jail it was the same way. Eat every day at the same time. Shit when it's your turn to shit. It got to where he depended on that kind of schedule, got lulled into it like a hammock he didn't even have to rock himself. Even now, on Tuesdays, he got a taste for green Jell-O, one of the surprise desserts they were allowed if no one had fucked up too bad.

It was anyone's guess where them two were headed, though. Maybe school, maybe not. He texted the both of them. He knew that Dayna bitch would get back to him, in one way or another, she was so grateful to have his attention.

"Jameson," his momma called. If she didn't see him right in front of her, she started calling his name. He could be three counties over, for all she knew. She'd just keep calling until he showed up, or until she gave herself a stroke.

Worse, she was calling his name with that little baby-doll voice, that voice he'd heard her use on any man she wanted something from, didn't matter if it was her son or just some crotch rocket she met at a bar. But her bar days were long gone, now that she couldn't hardly get herself out of bed or off the couch. So that voice was all for him.

"Jameson!" It was the kind of voice he wouldn't mind hearing from Perry, yearning, husky, afraid even. He walked quickly back, took the steps all at once.

"Jameson," she said when she saw him. She'd worked some lipstick out of that nearly empty tube she kept under the cushion, he could see how the orange smeared on her lips matched the orange all around the tip of her finger. "You'll rub my feet?"

If he said no, she'd make him regret it. On the occasions he did refuse, like when she wanted him to bathe her, or help her pick out an outfit she'd only be wearing to the couch, she'd thrown a tantrum she'd cooked up special for him, thrashing and yelling and even once flopping to the floor like all the life had gone out of her.

He had been a difficult son. He hadn't made it easy on her. Had abandoned her when he went to jail. He knew this was her way of paying him back. He hated the thing she'd become, this sickly whale, hated that he'd been any reason for it. One hate repulsed him, one drew him nearer.

"My feet?" she said, that squeaking in her voice, that sexual squeak; she was begging.

Sometimes he hated her for being weak enough to conceive him in the first place. "Just let me get the lotion," he told her.

"I have some," she said. That plump claw going under the cushion, her mouth wet, excited. "It's Jergens," she said, holding it out to him. He didn't know how she could lie comfortably with it stashed under her cushion like it was, but then again it was only one of many treasures she nested upon.

She hefted her legs up so he could sit, brought them down upon him. "Don't be no skimp," she said.

His momma's feet were soft, white, thick, and as unlined as a baby's. Ragged patches of polish dotted her toenails. He'd have to see about Perry's feet. Did she keep them up, or was she the kind to pay no mind to stuff like that? It suddenly felt very important. He squiggled some Jergens into his palm, began working it into the tops of his momma's feet. He tried not to watch his hands.

"I said don't be no skimp!" She swatted at his arm and missed. Jamey pressed harder. "Mm," she said, relaxing back into her cushion. "My boy's got strong hands, don't he?"

Jamey figured that Perry and Dayna must be at school by now, or still in the car on their way to somewhere, the windows down, air smelling like exhaust or biscuits or honeysuckle, depending on where they were. Here in his momma's trailer it smelled sour, the sourness of a woman who didn't move all that much, the sourness of her skin and breath and fear. The Jergens tendriled through, did its best. It smelled clean and plastic, and Jamey pretended like that was all there was to smell. He made another mound of lotion in his palm, ground it into his momma's feet.

"Why don't you have no girlfriend?" his momma asked. Her eyes were closed, the back of her hand across her forehead like she was bravely enduring whatever.

"How you know I don't?"

His momma snorted. "Okay," she said. "You don't want to tell me, that's fine. I'm just saying I know a man's got frustrations, and you ain't taking those frustrations out on me."

You wish, Jamey thought. She moved her toes, their sour smell familiar to Jamey, the definitive scent of his momma. He dumped on more Jergens.

"I'm working on it," he said. "I got my eye on someone. She's acting hard to get but I know she'll give in. She's nearly mine."

"Good," his momma said. "That's real good, baby." She flexed and pointed her toes, her voice that squeak again, that girlish hidden promise.

Jamey closed his eyes, tried to imagine it was Perry's feet he was working on. *She's nearly mine*, he thought again. He knew it was true, too, that it was flimsy, whatever was keeping Perry from him, delicate as a diary lock, and he just had to find the key. Or something proper to smash it with.

THEY WERE AT THE DRUGSTORE. Baby Girl had driven right past the school, right past the entrance to the highway, right past the turn they'd have to take if they wanted to hide out all day in the woods or hang out by the quarry. Plenty of kids did it—you just drove in as far as you could go, parked your car off the side of the road, and then plunged in on foot. If anyone was determined enough to drive in and go looking for someone, they'd only find your car, and they'd assume you was just someone who lived in one of the shacks or huts or tents way back there. Most people would assume, anyway. And then you'd just spend your whole day in there, sitting around, daring each other to run hard toward the quarry, and only stop just short of tumbling in, ha-ha, close one. Throw your old cigarette packs in, or someone's shoes if they were dumb enough to lose sight of them for a second. Perry wouldn't have minded going there, being outside, daring Baby Girl to lumber to the edge. But Baby Girl had kept driving.

"What you wanna do?" Perry asked her, three times, and each time Baby Girl just shrugged, but it was clear she had a plan. Hadn't even slowed in indecision. And then finally she'd pulled into the parking lot out front of the Walgreens.

"I got an idea," she said.

The plan was for Perry to distract the cashier. They were counting on the cashier being male, so Perry wouldn't have to work too hard to keep his attention. Just push her hair around, cross her arms so her shirt got tight over her chest, ask what time it is.

They'd walked in separately, Baby Girl about thirty seconds after Perry. Once inside, Perry saw that the cashier was an old woman, her hair a pink-tinged cloud, her mouth so beset with lines it looked like she'd once had her lips sewn shut and the scars had never healed. Perry texted Baby Girl: *This bitch looks mean.*

Itll be fine, Baby Girl texted back. *Go to plan B*. Plan B was for a female cashier. "Ask about pregnancy tests," Baby Girl had said. "Lady cashiers will either want to lecture you or else they'll want to take you in the bathroom, help you unzip, and pat your head while you pee on the stick."

She was in one of her moods, Perry could tell. Couldn't take her eyes off the goal, which Perry wasn't even clear on to begin with. Distract the cashier. Wait for Baby Girl to walk out. Wait for her cell to ring, pretend like it's urgent, walk out fast with her phone to her ear, get in the car.

But what was Baby Girl even doing? Obviously stealing something, but what? She'd find out soon enough, she figured.

A man was buying cigarettes. Perry waited behind him. She checked her phone, she shifted from foot to foot, she touched the packets of gum like they were jewels. She wanted the lady to see how nervous she was, wanted the lady to feel sorry for her. Didn't want the other option: getting a lecture about keeping her legs closed. She was surprised to realize the dread in her belly was real: it swirled and stabbed, it had a mouth with teeth.

The old woman finished with the man, looked at Perry with her eyebrows arched. They were mostly drawn on, Perry could now see, in a navy blue pencil. Her lips just lines of orange. Perry felt for the woman, all those colors that didn't go.

"You buying something?" the woman asked. "I can't sell you no cigarettes unless you got an I.D."

"No, ma'am," Perry said, using her best *I'm scared* voice. "I'm not a smoker."

"Not here to judge you," the woman said.

"Thank you, ma'am. No, I'm, I need help with, pregnancy tests?"

The woman watched her, those two orange lines moving like the woman was working her answer around in her mouth first, making it smooth and clean, before spitting it at Perry.

"I'm not saying I *am* pregnant," Perry said. "I just need to know."

Finally the woman answered. "Well," she said, "what do you need help with? Are you asking do we sell them?"

Perry hadn't prepared for this. The woman's eyes were pale blue, like they'd been put through the wash too many times. They glittered at Perry, watching her act like an idiot.

"I know you sell them," Perry said. She hoped it hadn't sounded too bitchy. Where in the hell was Baby Girl? "I'm just asking if you know which is the best one. And also what aisle?"

"Sweetheart," the woman said, but it was clear she didn't feel like Perry was no sweetheart. "I am seventy-two years old. When I was the age to have babies they didn't have no tests. You just waited for the doctor to nod or shake his head. Aisle three. As to which is the best brand, your guess is as good as mine."

"Well, thank you, I guess," Perry said, and this time she hoped it did sound bitchy. Fucking Baby Girl. Now Perry wasn't sure what to do. This woman had clearly dismissed her but her job was to distract the woman, not go off to aisle three and stare at the pregnancy tests. In fact, she hoped to never have to look at a pregnancy test, ever in her life.

"What else?" the woman asked. Perry looked at her nametag. *Mabel.*

"Well, *Mabel*," Perry said. "How about condoms? You got any advice on those?"

The woman laughed, so hard that Perry could see a gold crown at the back of her mouth.

"You got it backward, young lady. You should've asked about condoms a long time ago."

That was it. Perry would rather be at school, would rather be licking the floor of her math class than standing here getting lip from this old lady while Baby Girl did God knows what.

Perry picked up a slim pack of gum and threw it at the woman. It thumped her on the chest and fell to the floor. The woman flinched, made a sharp *oh* sound. "I guess I'll just buy this pack of gum and hope for the best, you old bitch." It was exactly what Baby Girl would have done. She felt like laughing.

The woman was reaching for the phone. "Need a manager up here," she said. "Repeat. Need a manager at the front cash register."

That was the last thing Perry needed. She turned and ran out the door to the car. Baby Girl had parked in the closest spot to the front door she could get, but the doors were locked. Perry crouched on the passenger side, hidden from the entrance. *Where the fuck are you???* she texted Baby Girl. *Come outside I fucked up we have to GO!!*

There was no answer. Perry stayed in her crouch. If she got up to run, it might be at the very moment the manager was coming out to find her. If she stayed put, there was a chance he'd just come out the front door, look around, go back inside when he didn't see anyone.

Perry checked her phone. Still no answer. Two minutes had passed, but it felt like two weeks. Her legs started to ache, she could feel her heartbeat behind her knees. It'd be second period now, English class. She hadn't read shit in the book they were studying. Still, she imagined herself in class, the sunlight coming through the windows all warm and friendly, her teacher waiting for answers instead of calling on people, Perry where she was supposed to be for once. Travis with his head down, taking notes. Travis.

She checked her phone again. Another two minutes gone, still nothing. Maybe there wasn't no cell service in that store, way in the back. If that's even where Baby Girl was. The parking lot was quiet. Every once in a while a car drove by, a rising sigh and then a hush. In the distance a siren was going, but it was so far away it was almost soothing. She shifted from a crouch to a sitting position, her butt on the hot asphalt of the parking lot, her legs filling with blood, a relief.

School was about a mile back, give or take. Her book bag was locked in Baby Girl's car. Oh well. It wasn't like she'd done any of her work anyway. Someone would let her borrow a pen and paper.

She was in the middle of texting Baby Girl *Fuck this, see you at school* when she realized the siren was getting closer, was practically on top of the drugstore. Right then it was all clear: Baby Girl had also fucked up, the cops were coming for her, would get Perry, too, if she didn't get going. She stood up, her legs stiff, her right foot all pins and needles. The car was already there, was pulling in on the driver's side of Baby Girl's car. Perry crouched down again, even though she knew she'd been seen, had looked right into the passenger seat of the cop car and met the cop's eyes, had looked long enough to see that the cop was a woman.

"Get that one, too," she heard Mabel yell. "She came with the bald one and assaulted me with some merchandise."

Perry stood, walked over to the lady cop. It felt good to walk after crouching for so long. And plus she knew that old lady cashier wouldn't expect her to, would be expecting her to try to run. And she'd be damned if she'd let that old bitch feel such a triumph.

The lady cop had a paunch, her zipper almost bursting with it. Flat-chested. Needed to pluck her eyebrows. Her partner, a man, was walking over to Mabel. The lady cop held her hand out, took Perry by the elbow. Her fingers were cool and firm. She opened the back door to the squad car, said, "Have a seat." Placed a gentle hand on the top of Perry's head, shut the door with a click as soon as Perry was settled.

Perry watched her walk inside. Her pants were too tight, her ass the shape of a pear. Perry still had her cell phone. The cop's hand on her head had been so gentle, so caring. She hadn't wanted Perry to hit her head, hadn't wanted her to feel that pain. Even though she deserved it, and at this thought Perry felt like she might cry, though no tears came, her throat revving and revving like a car with no gas.

JIM HAD HEARD the two delicate beeps of a text coming through, had been lying on the couch staring out the window, the TV on mute, a pretty Asian lady interviewing an old man in an apron the last time Jim cared to look. He rarely got texts. Myra didn't enjoy it and work usually called, unless it was one of the younger guards, hungover, too sheepish to ask with their own voice if Jim could take a shift. It was his day off, a whole twenty-four hours of not being there. So it was either a guard asking for his mercy, or it was Perry. Either way, he didn't want to know.

The man in the apron put a whole bag of spinach into a blender, topped that with an avalanche of fruit. The Asian woman's mouth opened wide, a shocked smile, how clever! Outside Jim could see a line of sky above his neighbor's trailer, had watched a patchy cloud move into that line and slowly out. Now it was just blue. Myra had gone off to work, he was alone. A wayward couch spring knuckled into his lower back, but if he worked it just right it felt almost like a massage.

He'd seen the look in Perry's eye that morning. Knew she didn't have any grand designs on being at school. *We're going to school*, Dayna had said. Like she wanted it to be true, or at least had wanted him to believe it.

Now the man appeared to be making a salsa. The Asian lady stared off, her lips in a tight smile, like she was listening to someone in the audience. Jim realized it was an infomercial, not the morning show like he'd originally thought. He got up, snapped off the TV. His lower back felt bruised, like the couch spring was inside him now, trying hard to burst out.

He checked his phone, saw Perry's text. *I'm getting arrested. I'm sorry.* It would be a while before he could convince himself to go outside, get into the truck, see what he could do about saving her.

THE SUN WAS COMING IN through the wall of windows facing out to the gas pumps like it was putting down ties, like the truck stop was just the east wall of a big-ass tent the sun was pitching. Normally Myra would have felt sick inside, like the sun had tentacles and they were messing with her stomach, mixing up the dregs of last night's beer, pushing on her gag reflex. Normally her eyes would have felt like they could pop out, into her hand, still throbbing.

But this morning was a mercy. The window cleaners had come the day before, so it was like there wasn't even any glass separating the inside from the outside, the sunshine warm but not hot, every car pulling in seeming to sparkle, the radio turned down just low enough. No one had even tried to pay with change, or traveler's checks, or a coupon for a different brand of truck stop. And Myra felt clearheaded, straight-backed, awake. Alive. Had made the doughnuts with extra care. Each one with the perfect amount of glaze or frosting or sprinkles. Put the stale ones in a basket by the cash register at twenty-five cents apiece. Pulled all the ice creams and cold drinks to the front of the cooler, wiped the door to the doughnut case in wide circles until there wasn't a fingerprint, not a smudge of frosting to be seen. Filled the change tray with money from her own wallet. Answered the phone by the second ring, every time. The day was a gift, a miracle even. Myra knew better than to let it pass by unappreciated.

When she finished her shift she'd get Jim a present. A candy bar or an ice cream. Maybe even get Perry something, too. A magazine.

A box of condoms. She laughed to herself. It was good to be able to laugh about shit that wasn't under your control. And she'd treat herself, too: a six-pack. She could already hear the way the bottles clinked against each other, could see the way the sun would catch the amber bottles just so. And why not? She'd drank the other night, had, with the help of her new friend, finished off all the beer in the fridge. And she felt like a new woman. So la-di-da, she thought to herself.

La-di-da. They were like magic words or something, because no sooner had Myra thought them than the man she'd been thinking of as well walked through the door, in a different sleeveless shirt this time, a blank electric blue. The electronic bells chimed and he stopped, half in and half out, looking up like he'd be able to see them up there.

"Well, hey, Pete," Myra called over to him. She was behind the counter, working at facing all the bills in the drawer the same way, organizing the coins into little even piles in their trays.

"Hey," he said, walking over. Myra could see that his shirt was the mesh kind, the kind football players wore, or bodybuilders. Or rednecks. He didn't seem surprised to see her, but then again she'd probably told him where she worked. Or he'd seen her before. This was the only truck stop on this side of the highway for miles. Why was she trying so hard to convince herself he hadn't been meaning to see her?

He was right at the counter now. Myra could smell lotion on him, Jergens, the same kind she used after a bath. He was the type to wear mesh sleeveless shirts and lotion himself up, an odd mix of vanities. It sent a little flare, a fiery wing, right up through her, knowing this about him.

"What can I do you for?" This was a saying she'd often heard Marshall use, a saying she hated. Marshall was the other cashier on busy mornings, a small man in huge glasses, his waxy fingers and effeminate voice also not doing him any favors. *What can I do you for?*

It was like his shield, stopped customers in their tracks, usually made them smile. And now Myra was using it. What had gotten into her? She was not attracted to this man, this pudgy boy, as far as she knew. But she also knew that she wanted *him* to be attracted to *her*.

"I'm just here for some gas," he said.

"And to see me?" she said, before she could stop herself. Still, it felt dangerous, the fun kind of dangerous, blurting things at this stranger. Seeing how he'd react.

"Well, of course," he said. He put his elbows on the counter, leaned over. A gold cross on a thin chain, a woman's necklace, really, spilled out of his shirt. In the clear light of day Myra could see how that cleft scar had made his upper lip look unnaturally full. She imagined kissing it, imagined it moving around her body like a bloated earthworm. She smiled to herself.

"You happy to see me?" he asked. Myra considered it. No, she didn't feel happy. His presence made her nervous, the way she used to feel before Jim, when every man that came through the truck stop seemed like a real possibility. She liked having that back in her life, Lord help her.

"Not as happy as you are to see me, I see," Myra answered, mirroring the close-lipped smile he wore, trying to look as confident as he did.

"I'm always happy to see pretty ladies," he said, tucking the cross back inside his shirt.

Myra laughed. "You're up to your elbows in bullshit, boy," she said, but she knew it was clear he'd flattered her. Breaking her down inch by inch. *Baby steps.* Who used to say that? Jim. About her not drinking. *Be patient, Myra. Baby steps.* Thinking of him now was like seeing a fly drowned in your beer glass. It tainted the whole thing. The light coming in through the windows even seemed dulled by it, less sharp, less pleasing.

Pete spoke, and Myra snapped out of it, though she hadn't heard him.

"I was asking if your daughter got to school this morning," he said.

"So she said," Myra answered. This man-boy was attracted to her daughter, that was clear. The thought didn't alarm Myra. If he wanted to try something with Perry he'd have another think coming. Instead, she was starting to feel put off, like she was the momma he had to be polite to in order to get anywhere with her daughter. Like she was just something he had to get past.

"You sure do like asking about my daughter," Myra said. Fun dangerous.

He backed up, straightened. "I'm just making small talk," he said. "Plus you said how you worry about her, how she lies all the time."

Myra didn't remember saying anything like that. She also didn't quite remember how she ended up in the bathtub, so it was possible. It was something she often thought about Perry, and so might very well confess it if she was relaxed enough. She walked from behind the counter, pretended to wipe down the doughnut case again. She wanted Pete to ask her about *her*, was what it really came down to. And because of that, she wanted him to leave. No longer the fun kind of dangerous, having these thoughts.

"These doughnuts sure do look good," he said. "They look like just the thing."

She didn't remember telling him she worked here. And yet here he was, stopping in for a visit. What else didn't she remember saying? Doing?

He moved toward her, putting his hand over her hand, which was on the door handle. He didn't even use the wax paper, just reached in with his bare hand and took a glazed and a strawberry frosted, put his finger through their holes and held them up, stacked one on top of the other. Myra didn't know if she was supposed to see something sexual in what he'd done, his finger in the holes, but she felt hot all over, she felt the flood of fever that always started a hangover. So here it was.

The phone was ringing, it was already past the second ring now. The sun had pulled up its ties. The truck stop looked dingy, tired. The smell of gasoline everywhere. The rag in Myra's hand felt oily. The mercy had been fleeting.

"Ain't you going to get that?" Pete asked.

She realized it was the perfect way to get rid of him, to answer the phone and tend to whoever it was with such thoroughness that he had no choice but to leave her to it. She walked around the counter, lifted up the receiver. "Byron's Truck Stop, Myra speaking," she said, forcing a shard of cheeriness into her voice.

"Myra, it's me," Jim said.

Now the fever spread into her hair, claiming her scalp. Jim never called her at work, not ever, he'd drive over sooner than he'd pick up the phone. She put her hand up to her mouth, she felt something coming and wanted to be able to hold it in. Pete took a bite from the stack on his finger.

"What's wrong?" she asked, that shard of cheeriness in her gut now, slicing her up. "Where is she?"

"Dayna got caught stealing," he said. "Perry threw something at a cashier. They're both in the holding tank."

His voice was flat, bored even, but Myra knew he was doing that for her benefit. Pete was at the counter now, obviously listening to her conversation. A blue sprinkle clung to his lip. Myra wanted to push it into the dent of his scar. Why wouldn't he leave?

"I'm on my way over there," Jim was saying. "You stay put. I'll take care of it."

"Let her stay there," Myra heard herself saying. "Let her stay there a night." The more she spoke, the more sure she felt about it.

Pete mouthed, *Where?* The sprinkle fell to the counter. *Arrested*, Myra mouthed back. She wanted to shock him, wanted him to leave her be. His mouth opened wide, like he was shocked *and* impressed.

"You don't mean that, Myra," Jim said, in the same bored voice. "It ain't a place for no teenage girl."

Pete had walked over to the doughnut case, was working the doughnuts off his finger and into a bag. Myra watched him fog the glass door with his breath, write *I O U* with his fingertip.

Fuck you, she wanted to say. Two birds with one stone. Instead she said, "I don't know what I mean."

Pete waved, walked out, the doughnut bag swinging from his fingers.

"I'll call you when I know more," Jim said, and hung up.

In those first few years with Jim, they never hung up without saying *Love you*. It was as natural, as automatic, as saying *Bye-bye*. They hadn't said it in years. Even so, every time they hung up Myra felt like something was missing, had been forgotten. And maybe that's why Jim never called her. He felt it, too.

A woman came in asking for baby wipes. At the counter she apologized, she only had quarters to pay with. Myra took them, dropped them into the tray, didn't even try to stack them. She felt something give, right then. It was just easier, not having to pretend like everything was finally wonderful. She threw the rag away, and that felt good, too.

JAMEY THREW THE BAG of doughnuts out the window of his momma's car. He could still feel the wax coating his mouth from the bite he'd taken earlier. Perry's momma was a freak. That farty smell coming off her: the beer seeping out her pores. The way she asked him questions that fed him the answers she wanted from him. *And to see me?* But it had paid off, he knew where Perry was, knew why Dayna hadn't ever texted him. They were busted, sitting in a holding cell, waiting on Daddy Jim to come save them. Probably watching some nasty hooker on the toilet. He pictured Dayna crying, her face in her shirt, and Perry refusing to meet anyone's eye, refusing to eat what food they pushed at her.

He felt closer to Perry than ever. It wasn't just coincidence that he was there when the call came in. He was meant to be there, meant to be staring into her momma's tired eyes as the news was delivered. They shared something now, he and Perry. He wondered did she feel the same helpless rage at being caged in, the same dedication to showing the guards she wasn't no idiot, saw right through them, was the smart one in the bunch. He was willing to bet that she did.

But she'd only be in there a few hours. And what with Jim being her daddy she'd probably never face charges, either. Jamey pulled into the parking lot out front of the courthouse. The holding cells were in the basement. He parked his car under a tree, the shade across his windshield, hiding him, so he could watch them come through the door.

And here was Jim now, walking out the doors, his hand on the back of his neck. No Perry, no Dayna. He watched Jim all the way till he was in his truck, all the way till he drove out of the parking lot, signaled, and was gone.

So maybe he did leave them there, after all, like Perry's momma had said. Left them there to think about what they done, stew in it overnight. Only then did Jamey recognize the relief he felt: He wouldn't have to decide whether to get out, pull his hat low, walk right past Jim. Dare him. The front of his pants got tight. Pretty soon he'd have to see about that.

BABY GIRL HAD SHAVED the rest of her head. Had taken cloth scissors and a men's razor in an orange plastic shell off the shelves, had walked into the back, into the employee bathroom, and set to work. What a stupid fucking thing to do. Real dramatic. And she'd even looked right at the lady at the pharmacy counter, saw the lady begin to smile, saw her notice the scissors and the razor, saw her face melt into the tired recognition that something wasn't right. Knew she'd been seen, kept walking anyway. Stupid.

But in the moment it had felt right, had felt like something that could scare people. Herself, even.

And now she had gotten what she asked for. She was scared. She and Perry were in a cell with three other women. Grown women. One of them was flat on her back, one arm across her eyes, her skirt bunched up so you could see that she wasn't wearing no underwear. What she had down there was bald also. Swollen and red. Mean.

It hadn't taken long, that was another shock. Just three chunky snips with the scissors, then a handful of neatly mown rows with the razor. Baby Girl had watched her own face as she worked, but nothing was all that different. Except she could see more of her face, there wasn't no hiding it. Her lips outlined in brown, like someone had taped a drawing of lips to her face. Like she was mouth first, everything else second. Her phone had gone off, a text coming in. She knew it was probably Perry, impatient as always, ready to go on to the next thing. But there wasn't no plan, Baby Girl didn't have no ideas. She'd cashed in her one big idea moments ago, her hair just a pile now, something she could leave behind. And then someone had banged on the door.

"Look," Perry said. She and Baby Girl were on their asses in the corner, so nothing and no one could get behind them. Perry nudged her, cocked her chin at the lady on her back.

"I fucking saw," Baby Girl whispered, shaking Perry's hand off her arm. When she'd gotten into the car next to Perry she'd seen that Perry was heaving, trying to cry, a sight she hadn't ever seen before. It felt like a gift or something, knowing Perry could feel bad enough to cry. Or at least to want to cry. *I texted Jim*, she'd said, her voice a screechy whisper.

But now there wasn't no sign of tears, fake or not. Perry had even managed to clean up all the mascara she'd rubbed into rings around her eyes, and it came to Baby Girl that the crying was just Perry feeling sorry for herself, not nothing deeper than that.

It had been a black cop at the door. "Make yourself decent and open this fucking door," he'd said. When Baby Girl opened the door she saw that he looked nicer than he sounded, and that he had pinkish bubbles in a cluster on one cheek. Zits. "I was going to clean this shit up," she told him, but it didn't matter, he took her by the elbow. Yanked her through the store.

"It fucking smells," Perry said. A homeless woman was in a lump in the corner, brown all over. The cell smelled like Charles when he forgot to wipe. Earlier a cockroach had come running out from behind her. Perry had smashed it with the heel of her foot, kicked it under the cot.

"You two whores?" This came from the third woman in the cell. She'd been braiding and unbraiding her hair, over and over, leaning against the bars. Bruises all over her legs and arms. "You two seem young, but then again I seen it all. You wouldn't believe it if I told you." The strap to her top kept falling down. If it could even be called a top. It was more like a dingy suggestion, an attempt.

"Yeah, we are," Perry said.

The woman on her back took her arm away from her eyes, propped herself up on her elbows. "No you ain't," she said.

"How you know?" Perry asked.

"Yeah, how you know?" Baby Girl said. She felt naked, revealed, sitting in this cell with her bald head. She'd expected it to grant her power, like a crystal ball or some shit. She couldn't let these women take over.

"You ever put your toe in a guy's asshole?" the woman on her back asked.

"You ever let a guy twist your arm behind your back while you're doing it?" the lady at the bars asked. "You ever let a guy use a flashlight on you?"

The woman on her back pushed up into a sitting position. "You ever been stabbed in the thigh and pretend to the next guy that you just on your period?"

"Jesus Christ," Baby Girl said. She couldn't help it. The women laughed, even the brown lump.

"How much?" the lady at the bars asked.

"How much what?" Perry asked.

"How much you charge? How much you do?"

"We do everything," Perry said. "Rates start at twenty-five to touch it."

The women laughed again. "Y'all must be poor as shit then," the woman at the bars said. "Ain't no one going to pay that much just for you to *touch it*." Her voice got whiny, imitating Perry.

"They do if you pretend like you twelve," the lady on the floor said. "That what y'all do? Show up sucking on a lollipop and twirling your hair and calling them Daddy?"

"This one don't even have no hair," the lump said.

"She makes more than I do," Perry said. "Because she's like a boy-girl. They love that shit."

"I'll bet," the lump answered, and all the women laughed.

Touch it. It. In Baby Girl's mind *it* was a weapon, an animal that could play dead till you weren't looking and then bam, you were in trouble. In her mind *it* was a tiny baseball bat, a bunless hot dog. It filled with blood when aroused, she had learned that in sex ed. A blood-filled hot-dog-shaped balloon animal. It was absurd, you could almost laugh if you weren't such a no-touching-it virgin. The extent of Baby Girl's experience was the time she had let one of Charles's friends take her for a ride on her own bicycle. She sat on the handle-bars while he teetered them through the neighborhood, winding farther and farther away from the house, until they were back where the new houses had started being built. Behind a yellow dune of sand the boy had reached under her shirt, pinched and twisted her nipples. You ain't wearing no bra, he'd said. Baby Girl hadn't known how to respond, what to say, had let him gently push her until she was diagonal, her back sinking into the dune, had let him unzip her jeans and reach down into her underwear and pinch and twist there, too. Had let him rest on top of her, had let him grind the hard front of his jeans into her until he shuddered and stopped and rolled off. Baby Girl wondered was he her boyfriend now, this boy she'd seen picking his nose, this boy who'd even farted in front of her, one morning after he'd stayed the night in Charles's bedroom. This boy who didn't seem like he'd be getting no taller, which was a shame. "Hey, look," the boy said. He was holding up a yellow rubber snake he'd found by the dune. He whipped it at her, hitting her on the arm. He laughed. The sky was pinkening behind him, the sting in her arm getting sharper before it began to wane. Baby Girl won-dered when the kissing would start, but he just hopped on her bike, barely waited for her to get on, too. Back at the house the boy had gone into Charles's room, and soon after, they'd left. Baby Girl watching television, working hard to focus on the program instead of the rawness she felt in her underwear. She and the boy never spoke about it and it never happened again. The next time she saw the boy he had his arm around a young black girl, twice his size. Then Charles had his accident and after that who the fuck cares about no boyfriend?

But it was like a shackle around her ankle, holding her back. Perry had done it plenty of times. Baby Girl hadn't done shit. Just that one afternoon in a dune when some boy had used her like a trash can.

"I don't even fuck them," Baby Girl said. "They just want to look at me. Because I'm a virgin." She was thinking of Jamey. How it had seemed like he might be the one to reveal it to her, might be the one to pick up where the boy at the dune had left off. How that made her a sucker, again, how she was that same dummy on the couch waiting to be undone by anything with a wiener. How Perry had her pick, just had to spin and point. How these ladies acted like it was nothing more than a garage sale. Suck you off for ten dollars, or best offer.

"No doubt," the woman on the floor said, and they all laughed, even Perry. For a quick flash of a second Baby Girl thought, *She belongs here.*

JIM DIDN'T HAVE no connections at the courthouse, or in the basement where they held people. Still, he was a guard at the prison, a kindred spirit of the law, and he figured it should count for something when he went to fetch Perry. Dayna, too, if they'd let him.

It was one of them quiet days. Everyone at school or work, blue sky, green grass, everyone making complete stops. A day when you'd tend to your yard, fall to sleep on the couch, wake up an hour later to see the sun still shining, just in a different spot. The peace of the day fell around Jim as quiet as snow on a frozen man. He appreciated it but it didn't help, the world kept turning, he was losing Perry and Myra and himself faster than he could get his head around. And he felt just tired enough to let it be.

Driving felt like something, though. He was taking action just by pressing the gas, pointing the car in the direction of the jail.

He knew he should feel angry, disappointed, betrayed. Embarrassed, ashamed. His stepdaughter arrested and him a prison guard. Ain't that something to yell about. He knew what feelings he was supposed to feel, he just didn't feel them. Maybe they'd rise to the surface after a while, like how dinosaur bones rise up after something shifts. He doubted it, though. First you'd have to have faith in the shift. Faith, something else buried.

He pulled in at the courthouse. The last time he'd been here was to marry Myra. Perry in ruffled socks. Myra holding a bouquet of silk flowers she'd bought at the Walmart, arranged herself. The lady judge jowly as a bulldog. Afterward they'd gone to the steakhouse for lunch, and together they'd decided to allow Perry to have as many bowls of ice cream as she could eat. Their first decision as parents was to let Perry do exactly as she wanted. And now look where she was. Jim tried to laugh, shook his head. It struck him that it was easy, back then, to keep his back straight. Like he was crafted from cement. Now it felt like a burden, rolling his shoulders back, making sure his weight was distributed properly. Easier these days just to lean into the world.

Did Perry remember that day? That must have been the last time she was here, too. But maybe they brought criminals in through a different entrance, maybe she had no clue this was the same place. She had called him Dad for a few years, but then one day it was Jim again. And if Jim was honest with himself he'd admit that it was a relief, that answering to that word had never felt natural.

Inside, a woman behind the front desk told him where to go. Had seemed disappointed in him, to be here on a weekday morning to see about someone who'd been arrested. She had a slur, her words coming out wet and slow, and Jim decided he couldn't be sure if it was disappointment with him or with how her own words landed.

Down two flights of stairs, the windows disappearing, the lights getting dimmer and dimmer. Through a metal detector and two sets of swinging doors. Into a waiting room where a Hispanic man and a woman in a head scarf sat rows apart. He walked up to the counter. A woman sat behind the Plexiglas on a stool set too low, scratching her head with a pencil.

"When was your loved one arrested?" she asked, moving the tip of the pencil to the back of her head.

"There's two of them," Jim said.

The woman pursed her lips, arched her eyebrows. Tapped her pencil on the glass. "When. Was. They. Arrested?"

"Just this morning," Jim answered. "About two hours ago."

"Oh," the woman said, "you can't do nothing until bail has been set. And I doubt bail has been set. You can sit here and wait or you can go home and wait, your choice."

Jim had his prison guard ID in his pocket, had planned to pull it out, slide it across, ask for a favor.

But now more than anything he wanted to get away from this woman, get away from the two people waiting, the woman in the scarf knitting and humming to herself, the Hispanic man sitting with his chest out, ankles crossed, doing nothing. Myra had said to leave her. It suddenly felt like the best thing for her, the best thing for the whole family. Certainly the best thing for Jim. He could come and get her in the morning. He could use the money hidden in an old box of Honey Smacks on top of the fridge to bail her and Dayna out. He could feel more prepared to look angry, to look like he cared.

EVERYONE HAD HER OWN SMELL in this cell. The hookers smelled like sex, like buttery sex threaded with fruity lotion. The homeless thing in the corner smelled like dirt, and like butt crack. Perry could smell herself, too: sweat and shampoo. And Baby Girl smelled the strongest, maybe because of how close she was sitting to Perry, but also maybe because she was losing her shit, and it was coming off her in acid waves. Like she was curdling.

Baby Girl looked like one sick bitch. Looked like she should be the mean one, but Perry could tell she was terrified. Like shaving off the rest of her hair had left her too exposed, all that armor fallen away, and now anyone could get at her. It was disappointing.

The cell was quiet now, the hooker without no panties had her arm back over her face, the standing one braiding her hair again. Baby Girl was cracking and recracking her knuckles. A guard had come by and told them they'd have their bail set in the afternoon.

Sometimes Perry looked around and saw she was somewhere she didn't want to be. Sometimes it was sudden and sometimes it was because she'd done shit to make it so. She could count on two fingers the number of times she was happy to end up in some backseat, but she couldn't say that she hadn't done everything she could to end up there. And like now. She hadn't meant for it to turn out the way it did. She'd wanted to go to school, even. But here she was. And when Perry found herself somewhere she didn't want to be, she rode it out until it was done, because it was the only thing to do. She felt the crying from before in her throat. If she started up again they'd eat her alive. Had to remember how if she was a wounded zebra, she wouldn't limp for shit. She'd carry on like all her legs still worked just fine. Kick another zebra's leg to shit, leave the animal there as an offering. *Her instead of me.*

"Hey," Perry whispered. "I seen who you were texting with the other day."

Baby Girl cracked her thumb. "So?" she whispered back.

"I'm just saying, he's been texting me, too. Talking to me online and shit. So it ain't like you're the only one."

Baby Girl cracked her wrist, said nothing.

"I think he's trying to get with me," Perry said. "Just based on how he talks to me. Does he say shit like that to you?"

"We talk about all kinds of shit, I don't know," Baby Girl said, and Perry knew by the way she said it that he had never texted *Oooh baby* to Baby Girl.

"Maybe we should both watch our asses," Perry said.

"Whatever. I got other friends aside from you."

Perry felt a tingling in her gut. Like she was winning at something. "So you're just friends?"

"I don't even know what he looks like," Baby Girl said. She whipped her head from shoulder to shoulder, working at cracking her neck.

"I might meet up with him one day," Perry said. "Unless you say you don't want me to."

"Y'all definitely ain't whores," the woman on the floor said. "Fighting over some boy? Y'all is just joyriders, am I right? Or what, you steal a lip gloss from the store?"

"Do whatever you want," Baby Girl said. She moved her hands to her head, kept them there like she was holding her scalp in place. Like that might disappear, too. Was she regretting it? The thought was enough to make Perry feel tender toward her.

"What's that feel like?" Perry asked. She reached up to touch for herself, but Baby Girl moved quick, slapped her hand away. The woman on the floor snickered. Perry's face felt hot; Baby Girl had embarrassed her in front of these women, made her seem like the one who wasn't in control.

"You know what?" Perry asked, putting a hand on Baby Girl's leg, as friendly as an aunt, holding firm so she couldn't be slapped away this time. "As your friend it's my duty to let you know that you look like a fucking retard."

Baby Girl's head snapped up, and Perry saw how quickly this brought tears to her eyes. She knew *retard* would do the trick. *Good*, she thought. *Maybe it'll wake her up*. The women laughed, and Perry felt a stitch of pride. She wanted Baby Girl to know she looked like someone to avoid, someone to back away from, and then from the safety of distance to feel sorry for. Like Charles.

Baby Girl yanked her leg free, still staring at Perry like she had three heads. A fat tear slid down her cheek. "You wrong," Baby Girl said, her voice loud. She was talking to the woman on the floor. "One of us *is* a whore."

The women laughed again. Perry joined along. "Yeah," she said, "and one of us just wishes she was." She almost felt closer to Baby Girl than ever, seeing her like this. Still, she moved away, crawled to the opposite corner. Left Baby Girl there to get ate up by whatever hungry animal, if that's how she wanted it.

LATELY IT WAS like evenings could get dark on you before you knew it. Blink and the sky had pulled up its denim blanket. It wouldn't get fully dark for a long time, that denim deepening slowly into navy, and Jamey hated the wait. Reminded him of the time between dinner and lights out, when there wasn't nothing to do but choose between boredom and trouble. And some nights you'd be elated to taste your own blood, nights when a bloody nose was better than one more night of writing letters or staring at the walls or rubbing yourself raw, pretending you didn't know your cellmate was watching.

And lately, what with his momma on the couch and Perry not two trailers over, it was getting harder and harder to choose boredom.

He'd waited for Jim to leave. He knew Myra was home. He'd gone around back so he could see through her kitchen window, and after a bit she appeared. Went to the fridge just like Jamey knew she would. *Like a moth to a flame* was what his momma always said about drunks, and about his own affliction.

Another shade of blue had appeared over the sky. Soon he'd go knock at the door, walk in before she could say otherwise. Visit a while. Wait for her head to bob. Then get what he came for. If he couldn't be with Perry tonight, he could be in her room instead, he could be among her things, he could leave something of himself behind. The thought of it was so real that it was almost like he was in her room already, not standing in the shadows outside an old man's trailer, looking in at Myra. He felt impatient for it, pushed himself into the light and around to the front of the trailer. Knocked two quick times.

"Come in," she called. Didn't even come to the door. Jamey smiled, knew the beer he'd watched her fetch hadn't been her first of the night.

"Why were you lurking out back?" she asked him once he'd stepped inside. The trailer felt warm and sticky, like it was a body that sweated.

"You must have mistook me for someone else, Miss Tipton," Jamey said. He put his hands in his pockets so she wouldn't see the shaking.

"No, it was you," she said. She held her bottle out to him. "Take this or get yourself a fresh one. If you take this one you got to get me a fresh one, so either way you'll find yourself in the kitchen." She laughed. The lights in the trailer making her skin as yellow as beer. Jamey felt a surge of hatred for her, giving into her nasty like that. Just like his own momma.

Another thing he had in common with Perry.

He waved her off. "You finish that one," he said. "I'll get me a fresh one and when you're done I'll get you a fresh one, too." He could hear himself starting to talk like her, could hear how he was even running his words together, like he was as drunk as she was. It was something he did when he wanted people to feel comfortable around him, to feel like they were just talking at themselves in a friendly mirror.

"You still didn't say why you were lurking outside, watching me get messed," she said to him once he sat down. "You scared of me?"

"A little," he told her. This was a woman who liked to get flirted with. Her hair had flattened since he'd last seen her at the truck stop, her lipstick was dry, caught in the lines of her lips, but she still expected to hear about herself. He could see where Perry got it from, this sloppy vanity. Only Perry deserved to be vain.

"I ain't attracted to you," she told him. She put a hand through her hair, made it worse. "And plus I'm married."

"Yeah?" Jamey said. "Then why you letting me in at all hours?"

"Something to do," she said. She finished her beer in two big swallows, waggled the empty bottle at him. "Next," she said. Jamey handed her his own beer. She took it from him with one hand, using her fingers to hold his hand still. She looked at him, her eyes glittery and drunken, her eyebrow raised. "Next?" she said, and Jamey knew she'd probably used this line before, when she was younger, getting the boys at the bar to buy her drink after drink, thrilling them with her touch.

"You tell me," Jamey said.

She laughed, the same loud caw she'd let loose at the truck stop. Her skin gathered at her neck. Jamey wanted to tell her what she looked like to him, which was old. He craved the sharp lines of Perry's chin and neck, no skin to gather at all. Even so, he hadn't been touched by any female aside from his mother in a long while, and he could feel parts of himself starting to pay attention.

Myra let him go. "I'm a very sexual person," she said, putting up her hand to catch a burp. "It just oozes out of me, I can't help it. In case you got the wrong idea."

"I understand," Jamey said. "But I still think you're a liar." He knew women like this needed to be challenged. Corrected. Seen through.

This seemed to delight her. "A liar, huh? Maybe you got me. But I still don't want nothing to do with you. I can flirt if I want to, no harm done there."

"That's okay, Miss Tipton," he said. His hands suddenly felt empty, purposeless, without a beer to hold on to. He leaned over, took Myra's foot in his hands, began rubbing her ankle the way his momma liked. Myra stiffened at first, but soon she melted back into the couch, closing her eyes, saying *Mmm*. Myra had bony ankles, creamy and smooth. Jamey wondered if Perry had the same ones. Jamey looked down the short hallway, toward the door he knew led to Perry's room, wondered how much longer.

"You ever been arrested?" she asked him.

Jamey stopped what he was doing. "What? Why you asking me that?" He almost yelled it. He'd been lulled into thinking she'd been lulled. He'd been nearly enjoying rubbing the ankles of a woman that wasn't his momma. Why wouldn't she just drop off?

Myra sat up, planting her feet on the carpet, rolling her shoulders like she was trying to wake her body up. "My daughter got arrested today," she said. "Oh, I told you that, right? When you just *happened* to stop by the truck stop. You see what I mean? You're like a bee in my bonnet. You want something, I just know it. And to be honest with you I'm nearly too tired to fight you off."

Now Jamey was the one who felt challenged, seen through. He put his hand on the knobby robe over her knee, pushed a little. If he said anything, tried to deny that he was always hanging around, *lurking* as she'd called it, he knew she'd have him, she'd know it was true. "I'm sorry to hear that about your daughter," he said. "Your daughter a bad seed or something?"

"I raised her right," Myra was saying. "She goes her own way, which is how I taught her. No one to blame but herself." She tipped her head back, finished the beer he'd handed her. Jamey watched the delicate veins in her neck moving with each swallow. Again Jamey's mind went to Perry's room, the possibilities there. He was with Myra and he was thinking of Perry. It had been a long time. Such a long, long time since there had been anything touching him, or anything for him to touch.

Myra dropped the bottle at her feet. "Why don't you do something, already?" she asked. She could barely get the words out. "What are you waiting for?"

It was like she was reading his mind, like she saw his need and was here to help. It repulsed him, it scared him, how much he wanted what she had to give. He stood, meaning to move away from her, pretend to go for another beer, anything to stop whatever it was that was happening, but she caught him, reached right up and held him steady by his belt buckle, her other hand a wild spider at his crotch.

"I can do this," she said. "Let me."

He pushed her hand but she held fast. "I know you're lonely like I am," she said. "I know what I'm doing."

And it was true, she knew what she was doing, at least more than any girl he'd been with in the past. She unzipped him quickly, her hand plunging in, strong and sure, kneading him and petting him until Jamey wanted to lean in and fuck that hand, hard, show that he was a man after all.

But in the next second her hand was gone, was up to her mouth, was catching the amber spurts of vomit she was trying so hard to hold in. She ran for the bathroom, catching her knee on the jamb, and after the door slammed Jamey heard her heaving into the toilet.

"I'm so sorry," she called to him. "I didn't eat nothing for dinner."

"It's okay, Miss Tipton," he called back, trying to stuff himself back behind the zipper. "I'll just see you later."

He opened and closed the front door loudly. Then he walked careful, quiet steps over to Perry's door. When he had shut himself in the darkness of her room he realized two things that nearly paralyzed him: he didn't have a plan for how to leave, and he still had his erection. *First things first*, he thought, and felt his way in the dark to her empty bed.

JIM CLOCKED OUT, drove home in the yellow morning. Walked through the front door like he was dragging chains. For a moment, even though he knew better, he saw Perry's shut door and thought she might be just beyond it, lying in bed or fixing to go out her window. Then he remembered: he'd need to check the cereal box on top of the fridge for money, need to call down to the courthouse to see if bail had been set. His body felt pummeled, like he'd been worked over and only now, hours after the beating, could his muscles relax into their ache.

The night before, he'd gotten a call asking him to fill in. One of the newer guards up and quit, said he couldn't come in no more. Jim hadn't blamed him. If he ever found something better himself, he might make the very same call. And it had been a relief, having somewhere to go. Not having to watch Myra drink herself silly while Perry slept in a jail cell. Myra was already three beers in by the time he'd left for his shift. He'd put his hand on the top of her head, in the same gentle way he remembered his father doing to him. "We got to do something about her," he'd said.

"She'll be fine," Myra had answered. Cheersed him. It used to be he could see through these spells Myra had, these bouts of harshness, see right through them to the pain she was feeling. Now he didn't know. Maybe she wasn't all that worried, and maybe he should quit worrying, too. Or pretending to worry. Doing his duty as a stepfather.

But she was drinking, right there in front of him. That counted for something. He'd kept his hand there on her head, leaned down to kiss her on the cheek. "We'll figure it out," he'd told her.

It made him feel better, anyway, saying it out loud. "Okay," she'd said.

The shift had gone by as they all did, some hours blurring into the next and some hours like listening to the second hand of a clock. Each time he'd looked in on Herman he'd tried to put on a friendly face, but the man never met his eye. Stayed hunched at his desk or curled facing the wall on his cot. It couldn't be helped, Jim decided. And at least now the prisoner knew just how far he'd be allowed to take it.

He'd eaten a cold sandwich at about three in the morning. Washed it down with inky coffee. The rest of his shift, the mixture burbled in his throat, bloomed into his mouth in hot, wet blasts. The desk guard and the other walker had just shrugged when he asked after Tums. He'd driven home as the sun was rising, thinking how he could breathe fire, wasn't that something.

Now he just wanted a shower. And there was Myra, flat on her back in the bathroom, a towel rolled up under her head. He'd seen the cluster of empties by the couch, had thought about having to brace himself as he walked through their bedroom door, but he thought he'd be able to shower first, that warm water soaking into his skin and soothing his muscles some before he'd have to tense them back up when he saw Myra.

She opened one eye, lifted her head, the skin on her neck collapsing in an accordion of flesh. "Jim?"

"Yes."

"I must have fallen asleep in here. I'm sick."

"I know."

"Am I ugly?" she asked him, pushing herself up on her elbows. "Is that why you're looking at me?"

"No, you ain't ugly." It was true. She was a beautiful woman when he'd met her, a tall woman with bright eyes and red lips. And she was still beautiful. Like how a prize garden that had gone to weed in a few corners was still beautiful.

"You know I like to keep myself up," she said. "I hate for you to see me this way. I got a little tipsy last night."

Jim felt impatient for his shower. He'd had this conversation with her so many times, in so many ways. If he yelled and stomped she'd only do it again, as soon as she could. He couldn't bring himself to muster the kind of energy he'd need to feel that angry about it anyway. And if he tried to reason with her she'd cry, beg his forgiveness, and he'd have to give it, repeating himself over and over, just to calm her down. Best to just let her talk. Help her off the floor. Ask if she wanted eggs. And then shut the door as soon as she was on the other side.

He held out his hand to her. She took it, pulling on him to stand. She held on to the tiny counter for balance, pushed her other hand through her hair to smooth it. There was a messy imprint of her eyelashes in dried mascara on her cheek, a cluster of black legs.

"I had a friend over," she said. "He kept getting me fresh ones. I didn't realize how much I was drinking."

This was new. Myra didn't have friends, not these days, and definitely not male ones. "He?" Jim said.

"This young kid from the neighborhood. He's got a crush. Sometimes I need someone to talk to when you ain't here at night."

Jim knew Myra liked to reach out, feel around, see if he still had buttons to push. Would he be jealous? Angry with her? Would he feel guilty that she needed to talk to some kid because he wasn't there, wasn't there a lot?

And he did feel angry, just a shade. Not because of how she was spending her time. That was so far down the list of shit he had to tend to with Myra that it nearly dropped off. He felt angry because he never, not once, got to just come home and get in the shower. First he had to make sure Myra was alive, drive Perry to school, and now go out and punch some neighbor kid for getting fresh on his own couch with his own wife, because it was what was expected of him.

She's lying, anyway. The thought came to him in blinking neon clarity. She was lying to get him to do something about it.

And now it dawned on him that she hadn't even asked about Perry, hadn't wondered what the plan was or if she could do anything to help. Had risen as empty as a scarecrow, filled the room with the brackish fumes of her breath. His body was so tight he felt like he could shatter.

"The other night a man asked me did I have a teenaged daughter," he said. "A prisoner. I popped him in the eye. It bled all over. It bled so much I felt sick. But I didn't even think twice, I just did it. You got a teenage daughter sitting in jail right now and you haven't done shit except invite some boy in to watch you get ugly."

Myra let go of the counter, stood as straight as she could. Put a shaking hand back up to her hair. "She's there because she wanted to be there," she said. "She knows right from wrong. It ain't my fault she acts the way she does."

It was what Myra always said. Jim could feel his heart pounding, his body hurt even more because of it.

"I'm going to take a shower," he said, put his hands on her shoulders to steer her out. "And go see about getting Perry out. If you make eggs I'll eat them. If you don't, that's okay too. Long as you get out of this bathroom and let me be."

"I touched him," Myra said. Her eyes moved back and forth rapidly across his face, searching for how this had landed. "I touched him where it counted and I would have kept touching him if my sickness hadn't overcome me."

Jim's hands felt like they might crack with how hard he was trying not to shake her. Instead he steered her out the door.

"If that's true," he said, "then I feel sorry for you."

"He liked it," Myra was saying, but Jim closed the door, pushed the little nub lock. "He liked it," she said louder, and slapped the door with the palm of her hand.

Jim turned on the shower and undressed. In the mirror he saw a man who looked like all the air got sucked out. The mirror slowly fogged over, and he was just a smear. A blur of a man, could be anyone.

Myra called to him through the door. "I can't hear you," he yelled back, but in truth he had heard her. *I wanted to be touching you*, she'd said.

But that was probably a lie as well. Finally, he stepped into the shower.

HE'D FALLEN ASLEEP in Perry's bed. Had put his mouth on the stiff part of her pillow, the part where she drooled, and drooled into it himself. Before that, had spit into his hand, meaning to touch himself, go for it, his cock still hard from Myra's touch, but he couldn't get up the nerve. It felt wrong, it felt like something he should be saving for her, not keeping all to himself. And it'd be all the more sweeter when it did happen, if he held off. He'd fallen asleep envisioning it: he and Perry in her room, in his room, on a bed of leaves in the woods somewhere, pulled off to the side of the road in the backseat of his momma's car.

Didn't wake until the morning, still hard as a rock. Jim just on the other side of the door and mad enough by the sound of it to kill a puppy. Perry had once told him that she snuck out her window at night. It was a sliding window, about three feet wide, and he knew it was his only chance. But his back felt glued to her bed, his limbs useless. If he moved they'd hear. Jim would beat on the door until the dresser Jamey had pushed in front of it gave way. He listened as they fought, not two feet away.

He liked it. Jamey heard how desperate she sounded, wanting Jim to get mad, probably wanting Jim to shake her, rip off her robe even, make her see who her man was. He'd read similar shit in his momma's paperbacks, romances with intense love scenes where the woman always ended up begging, apologizing, offering herself up in one way or another. Jim had handled it all wrong, shutting the door like that. He could've had himself a little something.

"I wanted to be touching you," he heard her say. She was crying now, and soon he heard the clink of bottles as she picked them up. He didn't believe that shit, not for a minute. She wanted to be touching *him*, her Pete.

He could smell toast burning, butter heating in a pan. So she was making Jim breakfast after all. Which meant she was at the far end of the trailer, in the kitchen. And the shower was still running, so that's where Jim was. Jamey pushed himself out of the bed, pulled his pants up. Slid the window open inch by inch, as gently as he could. Had nearly put one leg out before he remembered. He crawled to the door and pushed the dresser back to where it was. If anyone was listening they'd be able to hear it drag across the stiff carpet. Jamey felt his stomach in his throat at the thought. He heard the toaster pop, heard Myra getting a plate down. He went back to the window, got one leg and then the other out, jumped and landed in a crouch. He crawled, again, and didn't stand until he was two trailers down.

Out front of his momma's trailer he put his hand in his back pocket. What he found there sent a thrill so sharp he almost peed. There were her panties, right where he'd left them the night before, bunched and warm from his body. Would she miss them? Would she know someone had been there and taken them?

He hoped so.

WHEN BABY GIRL GOT HER PHONE BACK she saw that there were no new text messages from Jamey. She hadn't responded the day before when he'd texted to ask where she was. It felt like weeks ago, getting that text, driving over to Perry's, driving to the drugstore, worrying that not texting him back was too big a risk, like she was playing too hard to get. But now everything had changed. Even her car felt different, like someone much larger had been sitting in the driver's seat, like overnight she'd shrunk down to something else. Her bald scalp burning like a lidless eye. There was no way he'd consider being with her now. Touching her. If he'd ever even been considering it in the first place.

No, he'd just been texting her and chatting online with her so he could find out more about Perry, find out where they went, what they did. For a moment, early in the morning lying sleepless in that cell, she'd felt angry. Enraged and righteous. He'd gotten in, he'd planted a flag over her heart, she'd even helped him stake it in. She could have torched a city over it. Her whole body felt alive. But now, driving home alone in her car, she just felt exhausted. Thinking of her rage the night before, she nearly laughed. How could she think Jamey liking her was possible to begin with? That she even wanted it? *Quit acting like a girl.* She heard the words, heard Charles's voice, preaccident Charles. Any time she cried around him, he'd say it. She had been acting like a girl, carrying on with Jamey like some desperate airhead *girl*.

That morning one of the guards had called her a goon. *Hey, Blondie, get your goon, someone's here to take you home.* And it was true. She was a goon. Perry's goon. The word felt like a second name. If the guard had wanted to insult her, well, the guard had done the opposite. The guard had revealed her, reminded her. *Fuck this,* Baby Girl thought, though by *this* she couldn't tell if she meant everything— the guard, arrest, Perry, Jamey, her own sad vanity—or the nothing she was hoping to drive into.

It was Jim, waiting there for them, watching them come down the short hallway like he was just picking them up after school, hands deep in his pockets. Kept them there when Perry walked up, even as she put her arms around him.

"Y'all are lucky," he said quietly. "Since Dayna didn't technically steal anything the drugstore ain't pressing any charges. And the old woman you assaulted says the Lord told her she shouldn't press no charges, either."

Baby Girl watched to see if Perry would laugh at this, but she'd just nodded, her head down. Like she'd learned her lesson. And maybe she had, at some point in the night, maybe she'd also been lying sleepless, but Baby Girl doubted it. It was more likely she was just giving Jim what he wanted, pretending like she'd grown a conscience overnight. It had disgusted her, seeing Perry's bowed head like that, filled her belly like a fungus.

Now, in her car, she couldn't understand her disgust. This was the way Perry had always been. It had never bothered Baby Girl before and in fact Baby Girl had treasured this about her, had envied it, even. So then what was different? She worried it was her own pathetic softening. She wanted to be touched. She wanted a friend. She wanted, she wanted, she wanted. She *was* pathetic. *Girly.* She had to get her shit together. She couldn't blame Perry for being what she'd always been.

In the parking lot Jim had pulled Baby Girl aside, his hand firm on her shoulder. "I'd tell you to stay away from each other," he said, "if I felt like you'd listen, but I know you won't. You bring out the worst in each other, is what I believe."

Baby Girl shook off his hand, wanting to say something back, but the words caught in her throat.

"You want to keep going on like that," he said, "I guess that's how it'll go until something stops you. I hope this was the something for you."

He had put a hand on top of her head, just for a second, like he was checking to see if it was real, what she'd done to herself. "Is this you?" he'd asked. "Is it?" Then he'd gotten in his truck, waited for her and Perry to follow so he could drive Baby Girl to her car.

"Fuck yeah, it's me," she answered now. It was ten in the morning, everyone at work or school. There were no cars in the rearview, just her own eyes looking back. It dawned on her that a man must have driven her car to the impound lot, had likely pushed her seat back so he could fit. She hadn't shrunk in the night after all.

WHEN PERRY SAW JIM'S FACE she knew her momma must have had a doozy of a night. Then when Jim told her about the old lady not pressing charges because the Lord told her not to, Perry could feel a ghost of herself standing nearby, laughing. It was how she would normally have reacted. But Jim's face and the way he kept his hands in his pockets made her feel sick. Myra was an asshole. She herself was an asshole. They should be doomed to live together in that trailer, each driving the other to drink, or go out and throw shit at old ladies, until the end of time. Jim should be living with some woman who had a garden, could put her lipstick on straight, drank a beer only when it was rude not to. A woman that didn't have no kids, a woman that didn't need him so bad.

Sometimes Perry hated the understanding she and her momma had, especially when she remembered how that understanding came to be in the first place, remembered nights when Myra would bring a friend home to *play cards in the bedroom*, remembered nights when Myra would spit up, quick and deadpan as a baby, scoop it up in her cupped hand, remembered nights when Myra wanted to sleep fitted to Perry like a snail to its shell. Remembered how the trailer felt soggy with Myra—there wasn't nowhere to go. Tears enough to fill the baths she loved to take, and it was a wonder those tears weren't carbonated.

Perry had seen Baby Girl at school, she was chubby and freckled, with eyes the color of maple syrup, and she had a big brother that was nice to everyone, only he was dangerous, too. *You don't want him liking you*, Baby Girl had said. Perry felt in love with him, felt desperate to play cards in her bedroom with him. Then after his accident Baby Girl started wearing his shirts to school, stopped bringing her books to class, shaved half her head. And Perry felt in love with that, whatever it was Baby Girl was up to, wanted some of it for herself. That armor.

But it had grown from the inside out. She'd wanted to show Myra how she looked, so she'd made herself metal, shiny as a mirror. Learned all about playing cards in the backseat of whoever's car. Getting warmed through with beer. And going further than Myra ever had: never, ever, asking could she have a hug or a kiss, never asking Baby Girl to spend the night in her room because she felt lonely. Ignoring loneliness, finding other shit to do with her time than be lonely.

Backseats and stealing cars and throwing gum at an old lady was easier than being at home.

She'd always wondered what Jim's backseat or stealing cars was. Figured he had to have something. Maybe he went to a diner after work some mornings, flirted with a waitress. Maybe he didn't even go to work some nights, and went to the home of a woman who had a garden.

But seeing his face at the end of the hall that morning confirmed it: he didn't have shit. She and Myra were what he had. She'd tried to put her arms around him, let him know she felt grateful, but it wasn't something she usually did, and it had felt like hugging a telephone pole. There had been no give.

They'd dropped Baby Girl near her car. She hadn't turned to meet Perry's eye, had just walked down the row. Perry watched her thick back and bald head until she'd ducked into the driver's seat of her car, out of sight. The triumph Perry had felt the night before, revealing her secret about Jamey, felt shameful now. Worse than the triumph was that she'd needed to show those other women the power she held over Baby Girl. The power she held in the world: men wanted *her*.

Travis was right in not wanting her. And Baby Girl was right in not turning back.

"Myra told me to leave you there," Jim said. His voice sounded etched through, scratchy and raw. "But I made the choice to leave you there all on my own. That ain't no place for teenaged girls, hopefully you saw for yourself."

Perry nodded. She knew that's how Myra would react, it had been why she'd texted Jim instead of her own mother in the first place. Still, it burned hearing it, that Myra had decided to go home and drink herself into a stupor instead of . . . what? Standing outside the jail, calling Perry's name? Offering to sleep with whoever if they'd release her baby? Getting arrested herself, to keep Perry company?

This was Myra's voice she was hearing now, not her own, Myra's voice running down the list of nothings she could have done. Perry was an expert at channeling that voice, at making excuses.

"I'm sorry," Perry said, another thing her momma often said, but Perry wanted to mean it, wanted it so bad that she clenched down, molars grinding against each other until her ears rang.

"I ain't taking you home," Jim said. "Your momma's not right, and since you already missed a day of school I figure you should go in today."

"I haven't showered or nothing," Perry said. She tried to keep the whine out of her voice, but it was there.

"You can wash up at school," he said. "I know they got sinks there."

"My schoolbag is still in Baby—in Dayna's car."

"I don't care if you sit in class and do nothing," he said. "You ain't coming home right now."

Perry heard how he was trying to keep control of his voice, too, saw it in his grip on the steering wheel. She wondered did he ever think about putting his hands on her or Myra, shaking them, pushing them, hitting them until he felt better. Knuckles throbbing and bloody instead of throbbing and white, there in front of him on the steering wheel, him having to breathe through all that rage unspent. It made *her* feel better, thinking of him losing control like that. Like it was possible that everyone had something dark inside them, everyone had something they were barely controlling, even that nasty old lady at the drugstore, even Jim. Even anyone.

JAMEY'S MOMMA was perched on the edge of the couch, struggling to get her pants on without using her hands, since they were busy planting her firmly where she sat. Kicking her legs, her whole face wet with tears. A warbling sound burbled forth from her, surfacing like a fart in a bathtub, when she saw him come through the door. "I was fixing to go out and find you," she said, "just as soon as I could get dressed properly." It was a bright morning, the sun giving off the kind of light that made him feel like everything was going to be okay as he walked the short distance from where he'd hidden in Perry's room to his momma's trailer. He noticed things he'd never noticed before, like how the neighbor catty-corner to his momma had marigolds in a pot that were so yellow they were surely fake. Or how the neighbor next to that had a stained-glass butterfly hanging in the window. Such beautiful green wings that caught the light and gave it back in a way that he almost felt flirted with. Or how pretty the name of the road that snaked between the trailers was. Cinnamon Way. He'd never paid any attention to it before, but it had a ring to it. It was fun to say, and he did say it, letting his teeth linger over the starting s sound. The counselor at the jail had said Jamey's urges were wrong, were sins if you were the type to believe in God. But he had her panties, he'd smelled the sour spot on her pillow. Jim had his hands full with Myra. Everyone distracted that needed to be. Except him. He was as focused as a soldier. His pecker so hard and sure it could have divined water in the desert. All the signs were saying his urges were just right.

But then he saw his momma. Her face slick with snot and crying, her hair mashed on one side, riding the couch like a lazy hooker, trying to scoot on her pants. His pecker had shrunk so fast he felt like it had dissolved. "Let me help," he said, and that stilled her legs.

"Leave it. I don't need them on now." With effort she swung one leg and then the other so she could lie flat on her back. Jamey stood by like a spotter, though he'd long suspected if she did fall he'd edge out of the way as quick as a bobcat and let her splat splat splat.

"Okay?" he asked, still holding his hands up like he'd catch her.

"You can't do that to me, Jameson. You can't disappear on me. I got to know where you are at all times. I got to know you ain't out there prowling."

"Yes, ma'am," he said.

"If you can't find a proper girl—a woman—then I'm going to have to be enough for you, son. Enough woman in your life. You hear?" She had reached up, was holding on to his forearm so tight he was worried her nails would draw blood. "They said if you don't do right they'll take you right back in and there ain't nothing I can do for you then."

"You don't have to worry, Momma. I was just out carousing with the guys." The lie came easy, the phrase *carousing with the guys* something he'd surely heard on TV.

"I'm going to have to be enough," she said again. Her eyes so brown they looked red at the edges, the flimsy lashes clumped and wet. She looked like something beached, something wet through and struggling for oxygen.

"You are enough," he said, and removed her hand finger by finger from his arm, placed it on the fleshy rounded dune of her belly. She had always been a needy mother, had always fed upon his attention like a shark to the chum. "You want me to get the Jergens?" Had always demanded to be touched. The counselor had told him mothers weren't supposed to behave that way, weren't supposed to desire their son's touch the way they might a husband's, but it was all he knew. It had always been this way. He had been rubbing her feet, had been going higher at her demand, since he could remember.

"Just sit with me," she said, another sign from above that everything would be okay. She fell asleep fast, her mouth open wide to scrape in any air it could. He hid Perry's undies under his bed and signed on, waiting.

I WANTA MEET UP.

Finally Dayna had popped up online, and Jamey had jumped at the chance to talk to her, find out if they were out, where Perry was, if anything had changed. Find out if Perry had mentioned him, frightened in the cell, confiding in her friend, her one true wish coming finally clear: to meet this love-dumb stranger, this boy she'd been toying with for weeks.

Yeah? With me or with Perry too?

So she had mentioned him, Dayna knew he'd been talking to both of them. Probably knew he didn't want nothing to do with her, in a romantic way anyway, knew he was just in it to learn more about Perry.

Both of u. That ok?

He wanted her to feel like he hadn't only been talking to her to get to Perry. Wanted her to feel like he was in it for friendship, too. In a way, he was, he realized. She said shit that could shock you. She was interesting to talk to. And she had a car. Finally, she replied.

I shaved the rest of my hair off and I don't got time for you to pretend like you want to be my friend still. That ok?

Im not pretending, he wrote.

I like u

Whyd you shave off your hair??

And plus, Perry was more likely to meet up with him if she knew she had a friend nearby. This was something he'd learned over the years: girls felt better if they traveled in twos. He'd learned to make it work in his favor. Flirt with the homely one in the pair and it stirs something up, a kind of pride—they always knew they were the better choice in the pair—that they'd feel ashamed of, try to tamp down by ramping up the loyalty. Show the other girl she wasn't the jealous type, that she was the strong one, and fine, no problem, agreeing to take a walk, hoping with each step that he'd come after her, knowing the farther she walked that she'd had it wrong all along, feeling worse because of it, and more often than not this girl, this scorned dummy, walking home with a hot face and a throat full of tears. Leaving Jamey plenty of time with the friend, the girl he'd been after all along.

So handling two was fine by him. But anything more than that and shit got chaotic. Flirt with three and you seem like a perv, someone who could buy beer but never someone to take a ride with. Ignore one and flirt with the others and the third will be the one to bring up your cleft lip, your gut, your outdated jeans.

I don't know why, she replied.

I just did it

Im sure u look real tuff, he wrote.

Aint nobody mess with u now

Right?

Dayna was another type of girl, one he had to keep on his toes around. The type of girl to dare you to think exactly what anyone would think if they saw a bald girl in boys' clothing charging toward them: *What the fuck is* that? She was downright begging for it, waiting for you to make a face or let out a *Damn, girl!* so she could stomp a mudhole in you, slice you up with her sharp tongue. Say how she had to get back before Perry could even get out of the car, drive them both away faster than you could pop open the beer you'd brought for them.

She might even hate you more if you said how pretty she looked, said how you always wanted to be with a bald woman, see what it was like.

He had to walk a fine line. Had to flirt with her only so far, had to make up the rest in pretend respect and pretend fear.

No one messed with me before

Why you want to meet up?

I wanta get to know u gals in person, he wrote.

He pounded the desk. Ain't no one in high school using the word *gals*. He'd never even really used it, it was something his momma said. *Why don't you bring any gals around?* He looked over at his momma now, cuddling the TV remote to her neck like it was a teddy bear, her eyes half-closed, which meant she was close to asleep. She looked like someone's doll baby that grew up and never lost none of its puffy rings of flesh, its blue-white skin, its half-lidded eyes. She hadn't been stirred by his pounding on the desk, a blessing. Quickly, he wrote:

I get lonly

Lonley

However u spel it

It was a risk. No telling if a girl like Dayna would feel disgusted at this kind of confession, or would soften, feel sorry for him, want to help him out. He knew Dayna was a good speller, hoped that acknowledging his own poor spelling would help to thaw her.

There are red squiggly lines that let you know if something you wrote is all fucked up and misspelled

You just right-click and choose the word you meant

Awsome, thanks

I see what u mean

Neat trick

He didn't know what she meant by right-clicking. Didn't care. She was like one of his teachers in school, acting like everything was so easy to understand, and he was just being stubborn. He wanted to tell her to forget it. It wasn't worth all this ass-kissing he had to do to get her to do what he wanted, he'd just work Perry harder, maybe even climb in her window one night.

Sorry you get lonely

I'll see if Perry wants to meet up

It had worked. She was the type of girl, he now knew, to feel flattered by confessions. To feel like she alone was worth confiding in. Probably because she felt like she had endured more pain than Perry, had more character. And it might be true, but Jamey didn't give a shit. Perry was the one with the blond ponytail, the grass-green eyes, the criminal's heart. He was pretty sure about that last one, anyway. It was a crucial part of the equation that made up the girl he was looking for: it meant she was up for anything.

Thank u

I mean thank you

We'll have a good time, dont worry

I'm not worried, she wrote.

Dayna has signed off.

He hadn't been lying when he'd confessed to getting lonely. He'd never been good at loneliness. Especially now that he was home, and home meant his momma watching him with her flat doll's eyes, eyes filled half with indifference and half with desperate suckling need. In jail he would have called his loneliness *boredom*. But now, outside, he saw it for what it was. He needed to put his hands on something, again. He'd start with his hands, see where it went. Some girls just went with it. Some did and then didn't. Some made him work for his reward.

He knew it was disgusting, wrong, this kind of need. He knew because it was the same kind of need he watched pulsing out from his momma. But it was beyond him. It was biological. It was instinct. As natural as a lion feeding off some thrashing animal, fighting hard to stay alive even as its belly opened up. That lion probably didn't feel all that great listening to the animal howl and die. But a lion's got to eat.

PERRY COULD SMELL HERSELF. It was the same odor she'd smelled all night, lying in that cell, coming off those women in waves. Crotch, left too long without a washrag. Salt, sweat, and something nasty, something nastier than sex, something hot and close like blood. Now she was the one with her skirt hiked up over her hips, now she was the brown lump wearing three layers of clothing, dirt on her face and lining her nails. Now she was the one trying to braid her hair like nothing, like there wasn't no smell, and if there was it was your problem, not hers.

She'd gone straight to class, hadn't stopped to wash up first, and now she regretted it. A girl had let her have a piece of paper, but no one had a pen for her to borrow. Without something to concentrate on, the smell seemed to be getting worse. A boy in the next row shifted, turning away from her; the girl in front of her leaned forward, hunched over her work. Everyone probably trying to breathe with their mouths, so as not to whiff in any more of her.

The only saving grace was that Travis wasn't in class. Perry looked over at his empty chair, glad that he wasn't there to catch a whiff.

She raised her hand, asked if she could go to the bathroom. The teacher nodded, waved her off. As she stood, a fresh burst of the smell bloomed out.

In the bathroom, she smelled her hair, her hands, her clothing. Went into a stall and put a hand into her underwear, brought it up to her nose and inhaled. She smelled stale, unwashed, like her body would smell if she stopped caring. Her hair still held a whisper of the fruity shampoo she'd used the morning before. Her armpits smelled mostly like the baby powder in her deodorant, only a small oniony fang of B.O. peeking through. Nowhere could she find the source of the crotch smell, but she still smelled it anytime she moved. Like it was the sum of all her parts. Like as a whole she was no better than a hooker's unwashed vagina.

She washed everything anyway. Soaped up her hands and worked the pink lather into her face, her neck, her armpits. Soaped up a wad of toilet tissue and pushed it into her underwear, wiping. When she was done she stood in a stall, letting the air cool her dry. Someone had written SLOPPY CUNT in red marker, the only words in this stall. If she'd had her book bag she'd have taken out a pen and written YEP.

In the hall she felt cleaner, more awake, her neck and hands cool. The soap she'd used smelled like bubble gum and toilet cleaner; she breathed in, hoping to smell it on herself, nearly happy enough to laugh when she did. There was even a pen on the floor by the drinking fountain. As she bent for it she heard footsteps coming around the corner, stood up just in time to see it was Travis.

"You weren't in class," she said.

He still had on his work uniform, and there was a deep line in his hair from where he'd worn his visor. Perry could smell the dishes on him.

"I'm sorry," he said.

"You don't have to be sorry. I was just hoping to see you." In the mirror Perry had seen that her hair was limp, flattened, all the shine gone out of it. She was glad, it felt like a miracle, that she'd pulled it into a ponytail before running into Travis.

"I'm sorry," he said again. He picked at his shirt, drips of grease dotting it like raindrops. "I mean, I meant, did I miss anything?"

"I want to kiss you again," Perry said. She took a step toward him, she couldn't help it, she wanted to be near to him.

"I know," he said, stepping back from her. "Me, too."

It was a shock, a literal shock, like someone had fastened a clamp over her heart and pushed a pedal that sent a current right into her body, up through her throat and down to her toes. He'd said he wanted to kiss her, too. Perry felt filled up, like someone had poured a kettle of hot water over her head. But he'd also backed away. Here came the hideous smell again.

"Maybe I'll stop by again," she said, "if you're working."

"No," he said, "don't do that."

He'd said it quickly, like the idea repulsed him. "Oh," Perry started to say.

"Meet me somewhere else," he said. "Tomorrow night I'm off. We can meet at my house or something. My mom works nights."

"I can do that. I can take the bus. I'll meet you there, if you tell me the address."

"Thirteen forty-six Baton Rouge," he said. "Take the bus to White Road and then walk into the neighborhood behind the 7-Eleven." She repeated it back to him, twice, trying to stamp it deep in her memory. The smell was cascading off her, she half expected to see it pouring over him like candle wax, but he asked her to come over, he gave her an address, and it was like he couldn't smell her at all. She wondered if she'd even tell him about her night in that cell, tell him about the other women.

"I'm going to skip this class," he said. "So I'll just see you later."

This was a relief. Perry hadn't wanted to walk back with him, hadn't wanted to break the spell, do something to change his mind. Hadn't wanted to walk into class with him, either, didn't want anyone thinking she'd gone to the bathroom to meet up with him. Not that she hadn't done something like that before. She just didn't want anyone thinking it about him.

And she didn't want him thinking anything like that about her. In the night she'd thought how it could be something she had pride in, that she'd survived all those hours in that cell. That she'd thrived, even. But now she felt ashamed even thinking about telling Travis about the drugstore, the jail cell, the other women. She watched him walk down the hall. His shirt was wrinkled, and a bit of it had come untucked, but it fit tight across his shoulders. So it was settled: She wouldn't say shit to him about her night. She'd pretend like it never happened.

CHARLES WAS STILL IN BED when Baby Girl got home, which meant their uncle hadn't been home, or if he had, hadn't noticed that Baby Girl wasn't home to make sure Charles got up when he was supposed to. She'd left him in there, not wanting him to see her bald head yet, not wanting to answer when he asked where she'd been. Instead, she'd gotten online. She wanted, more than anything, to show Jamey that she didn't care that he was only into Perry, that she'd just wanted to be his friend all along, she'd never been interested. She'd nearly convinced herself of it, driving home. She even started feeling sorry for him, how he tried to convince her that he really did want her to come along on the meet-up, how he confessed that he was lonely. He had no idea who he was talking to now. He had no idea things had changed, she had the power, and she would do everything she could to make him see that she was beyond caring about him. He wanted Perry, he could have her. He would see that any hold he had on Baby Girl's emotions had dropped away, as mean as a rock slide.

And Perry would see it, too.

After she signed off, she went to Charles's door and pushed it open. He was flat on his back, eyes open, his hands folded over his shirtless chest. He'd once seemed rock solid to Baby Girl, but now he'd gone all soft and pale, his nipples almost womanly with how fleshy they were, how they drooped whenever he stood.

"I think it's time for me to get up," he said. "My butt hurts."

He was upset, Baby Girl could tell. He was talking to her like she was going around the room and stealing all his things, right there in front of him, while he lay helpless on his back.

"You know how to read a clock, Charles," she said. "You know what time you need to be up. You don't need me to come in and get you, do you?"

His room smelled like breath. "But you always do," he said.

"Well, if I ever don't, like this morning, you got to be able to get yourself up. Okay?"

"Yeah," he said. "My butt hurts."

"Get up, then."

He swung his legs around. His boxers were loose and Baby Girl looked away so she wouldn't see his stuff, but it didn't matter. When he stood his thing peeked out the front, shriveled and brown-pink. Charles had had plenty of girls before his accident. Some of them had tried to be nice to her, offering up lip glosses and gum and, once, a pink condom in a glitter wrapper. They'd come and gone. Baby Girl had heard some of what went on in Charles's bedroom, girls moaning or laughing or yelling. It had made her feel sick, scared even, she couldn't see the point in it all. But now, in his bedroom on this morning, there wasn't no sex in what dangled from his boxers that Baby Girl could see.

Why did she have to always remember how he used to be? The doctors had said some days would be better than others. Some days he'd be a five-year-old, some days he'd be like an eighth-grader. But he'd never be the same person he was before the accident. And it wasn't like Baby Girl was waiting for him to be, waiting for some miracle to alight on his head like some kind of mercy bird. It was just that now she knew: there wasn't no point. You just did shit and waited to see what happened. Charles's accident had been like a line in the sand. And Baby Girl had crossed it over and over.

"Get dressed," she told Charles. "I'm going to take a shower, and then later I'll take you to the library."

They had adult programs there, mostly for homeless people, but Charles loved it. Those were his friends now, some of them with child brains like his. And it was somewhere she could leave him while she and Perry met up with Jamey. She could leave him home watching videos, make him a sandwich and chips to eat on the couch, but he'd been left alone too long already, because of her. Because she wanted to go out and shave her head in a drugstore bathroom just to show the world how little she gave a fuck. Now she saw that the fact that she wanted to show the world anything meant she gave a fuck, way too much of a fuck.

"You look like a boy," Charles said. "All your hair's gone. You have boy hair."

"Isn't it cool?" Baby Girl said. If she put the right tone into her voice Charles would go along with anything.

"Cool for a boy," he said. "You're ugly now. You're ugly! You're ugly!" He was jumping up and down, nipples jiggling, his thing flying up and down, over and over. Baby Girl could feel her face getting hot, the way it did when she was about to say something. "You're ugly ugly," he yelled. "Boys don't want girls who look like boys!"

Her head felt hot enough to pop. She ran at him, pushing her hands into his chest as hard as she could, until he was on his back on the bed. He wasn't her big brother anymore. She wanted to murder whatever he was now, wanted to crush it in her fists. If the real Charles wasn't ever coming back, why did she have to see his face every day?

His boxers had come all the way down in the struggle, and Baby Girl could see that he was hardening. She thought of the women in the cell, of Perry laughing with them, at her. Of the boy in the dune and Jamey. Charles before his accident, Charles now with what old

Charles would have called a chubby. Dicks everywhere, none for her. *You look like a fucking retard.* She slapped his face. "You're a fucking retard," she yelled, spit flying from her mouth.

He held his face, one hand on top of the other. He opened his mouth, his lips wet, and wailed like something was broken. Maybe his heart. She backed away, kept moving until she was safely in the bathroom with the door closed. Turned the shower on and stood under it so she wouldn't have to hear him carrying on.

She shampooed her bald head, her hands moving slow. Rinsed and lathered again. And again, hoping her heart would stop throwing itself against her rib cage. Tried to focus on how already there was some stubble, how she wouldn't look this way forever. What would Jamey think when he saw her? She couldn't stop herself from wondering. Such a pussy. The shampoo ran down her face until her eyes stung. *Good.* If she'd been teetering on the edge of ugly before she shaved her head, now she had definitely crossed over that edge. *Good.* There were new truths on this side of the edge. Like how you could stop caring what people thought if you knew there was no hope to look otherwise. Like how people might underestimate you, think you couldn't keep up. She held her eyes open under the water. She could keep up. She was way ahead, in fact. She would bring Charles's gun to the meet-up. Pictured Perry's face, how scared it'd make her, how Jamey might realize he'd underestimated her. It wasn't loaded, but a gun's a gun. She'd still have the upper hand. All along she'd been trying to convince herself she was stone all the way through. When she already knew that it was a fact, could feel the cold rock under the washrag she dragged over her body. This lumpy stone no one wanted to fuck.

IT WASN'T UNTIL AFTER Myra had eaten the eggs she'd made for Jim and then thrown them up that she realized she had a shift, and it had started an hour before. She'd called the truck stop, didn't even have to try to sound like she was sick, a small blessing.

"Myra," Bill had said, "why don't you take some time. Come back to us after you get yourself under control."

His voice was quiet and kind, pitying. The receiver smelled like Myra's breath: bile and eggs and the ruined yeast smell of beer. She wanted to get off this phone and stick her head in the fridge, the freezer, both at once, anything to get fresh air on her face.

"I got myself under control, Bill. We had some bad news about Perry yesterday, and I . . ." She couldn't say *drank too much*. Felt like too much of a give. So instead she said, "Ain't you ever made a mistake?"

"I knew you back when," he said. And it was true: they'd gone to the same high school, back when Myra was runner-up for prom queen and so God-fearing that she'd only sip from the beers handed to her. Never finish them. But she'd also gotten pregnant not two seconds out of high school, and she'd never made her way out of this town except to give birth to Perry at the hospital in the next county over, Perry's daddy long gone by then. So if he was implying those were the glory days, that Myra should look to them as blueprints for who she should try to be today, he had another think coming.

"Fuck you, Bill," Myra said. Saying it aloud felt like a drink from an ice-cold glass of orange juice. A blast of awakeness, the sky was blue, the sun was yellow, the fucking chimes tinkling just so, it was morning.

"Mm-hmm," Bill answered. "Take a week, dry out." *Click*, he'd hung up.

She looked in the fridge: no orange juice. But the cool air did help for a minute, and there was beer, one single frosty can so close to the shelf edge it was like it was daring itself to go over. She had no idea when Jim would be home, no idea if he'd have Perry with him. An image flashed across her mind, quick and dark and flickering, like she was watching it in a dingy movie theater: her hand on that boy's pants front. The feel of him, hard and sure, leaning in. The thought sent fingers of shame up her body. She'd have had him, if. And she'd told Jim about it because she'd been proud, proud that a young man wanted to fuck her: wilted, drunk her. Even now she felt a tingling down there. The fact was she was the kind of woman who would do the whole world, if it'd keep her company when she needed it.

She opened the beer, popped the top expertly with one finger. Gargled the first gulp and spat, the bubbles sharp and cold in her throat, her throat alive.

She was on the steps with her can, still in her nightdress, when Jim pulled up. She could see that he was alone, no Perry. The beer had sorted her out, organized her emotions and sickness into neat compartments, laid a fuzzy blanket over them. The sky had changed colors, it was a golden gray now. A storm was coming. They hadn't had one in weeks. Myra wanted to feel the first drop splash onto her face, wanted to tempt the lightning.

Jim walked over and stood in front of her, his eyes on the empty beer can dangling from her fingers. "I dropped her at school," he finally said.

"Good. It's going to storm, looks like."

"How come you didn't ask?"

"What?"

"How come you didn't ask where Perry was?" He was playing with his keys, clenching them tight and then letting them loose. Metal on metal, a terrible worrying sound.

"I would have gotten around to it," Myra said. "And besides, I figured she was in jail or with you."

She knew she was taunting him now, trying to push his buttons. Trying to piss him off. Give him just what he wanted: a drunken wife that didn't care whether her family lived or died. The fact was she had been worried about Perry, she'd been worried about her since the day she was born, worried so hard that she'd made herself sick, worried herself to the fridge night after night, worried until she convinced herself all she could do was trust that she'd raised a human being and not a monster. After Myra got boobs, her own momma started looking at her funny, asking to smell her breath, her neck, her hands. *You're going straight to hell to bear the spawn of Satan. See how you like the boys then.* And look how good all that worry had worked on Myra.

"I don't want her hanging out with that Dayna no more," Jim said.

He wasn't taking the bait, wouldn't scream at her about what a horrible momma she was, wouldn't even threaten to leave. Myra wanted to throw her arms around his neck. But that kind of action would require a trip around the world, a magic trick, some impossible kind of journey that Myra didn't think she was capable of.

"All right," she said. "But you know we can't control who she's friends with at school."

"She shaved all her hair off," Jim said. "Dayna did, I mean."

"Now that's a girl with some secrets," Myra said. "We can't blame her for that. Plus, with a friend who looks like that, the boys will probably stay far away, right? And I know for a fact that Perry ain't been talking to the boy she was into online, not for a while, anyway."

"What boy?"

"Just some new boy in town named James or something," Myra said. "Jamey. He likes bass fishing. For a while Perry would be on that computer for hours, talking to him. But all that stopped about a week ago. She ain't been on the computer in days, so she ain't replaced him with another, either. See? You think I don't pay attention, but I do."

Jim nodded. "Jamey, huh? Bass fishing."

"He seemed like a nerd type, as far as I could tell. Maybe Perry just liked the attention." Myra felt silly saying that last part. Might as well have been talking about herself, dredging up the fight she and Jim had that morning. Her head zinged at the memory of it, her hangover finally emerging from out of the fuzzy blanket. Her hand on that boy's crotch. Shame and desire. Storm. Her hand.

"Anyway," Jim said, sitting beside her. Myra knew he was thinking of what she'd confessed, too. "I got another shift tonight."

"I know," Myra said. "I saw on the calendar. I got a week off from work, courtesy of Bill." She didn't want to tell him the part about drying out, but it came out anyway. "He told me to get myself together," she said.

"Better him than me," Jim said. An attempt at a joke, a nod at their fights, and even though he was hinting at a mountain of pain between them, Myra felt thankful. Thankful that he'd joke, thankful that he knew her so well, thankful that he was sitting on the steps with her, him shaven and clean and her wrinkled and used up.

A low growl rolled over them, the thunder far off but closing in, the sky more gray than yellow now. The neighbor's chimes blasted, the wind picking up. Myra realized she hadn't heard the loud polka music in days, realized she'd take that over those chimes in a heartbeat. At least the polka was music, and not just a series of random screeching notes. With one you knew what to expect. With the other you just had to take what you got.

"We should get inside," Jim said.

"You go ahead," Myra said. "I'll be in after a while."

She wanted to wait and see if Pete would show up, wanted to tell him not to come by no more. The odds of him wandering around in a storm seemed slim, and maybe that was why it was so easy for Myra to sit out there, waiting to do the right thing. Wouldn't be her fault if she never got the chance.

BABY GIRL DROVE TO SCHOOL, waited in the parking lot for Perry. She'd sent two texts: *Hey bitch I'm in the parking lot* and *We'll meet you by the quarry tonight.*

She had left Charles at home after all. No library for him. Goon, goon, she was a goon. The gun was under her seat. All of it felt like a giant fucking joke. *I'ma get mine. I'ma get mine. I'ma get mine.*

She could see how it would go: They'd pull up, Jamey would be waiting there, he'd probably be cute enough for Perry to take over from there. Which meant he'd have a face and two arms and two legs, ha-ha. Maybe she'd show them the gun, maybe she'd keep it to herself. Depending on whether she wanted them to get scared or not. Depending on whether she wanted to get scared, too.

What had Charles done with the gun before the accident? Had he ever pulled it? Had he ever shot it? In her head she put the gun in the hands of the Charles he was now. He shook it, waved it around, laughing, pulling the trigger over and over, yelling, *Click! Click! Click!* right along with it.

She'd seen preaccident Charles get angry, saw how he could get as big and senseless as a gorilla. In her head, that Charles gritted his teeth, pulled the trigger, *blam blam blam*, three starbursts, aimed right at her.

She couldn't say which version of Charles seemed sillier. Both dancing apes, *Look at my gun!*

The parking lot security guard was headed her way, though she couldn't tell if she'd been seen. Today it was the PE coach in the golf cart, driving slow, peering and squinting into every back window. Baby Girl slid down in her seat. The sky filled her windshield, a wash of greenish yellow-gray. A few leaves blew by. She had the urge to honk her horn, over and over, come and get me, do whatever you have to, I don't know anymore, I don't know anymore.

Well, if she did show them the gun she'd make sure it was for a reason. But why had she brought it? Charles had once told her that if you pull a gun you'd better be ready to kill. She didn't want to kill. She just wanted them to stop breathing, ha-ha.

The golf cart was getting closer, moving so slow that Baby Girl had another urge, the urge to leap out and take off running, just to show the coach that she could outrun him, that he'd have been better off on foot. She pulled the gun out from under her seat, rested it in her lap. If he found her he'd be getting a show, that was for sure.

One day she wouldn't live with Charles no more, she wouldn't be friends with Perry, she'd be someone else with hair and a job and a memory of the day she sat in the parking lot at school with an unloaded gun. She heard the golf cart creep by her car, heard it reaching the end of the row and turning down another. So she hadn't been seen. More thunder, closer now, louder. She cracked her window. The air was thick, the sky like an overstuffed balloon, one more drop of water and the whole thing would burst.

PERRY WAS SURPRISED by Baby Girl's text, figured they'd had enough of each other for a while. But now here she was, ready to pick Perry up from school and take her wherever. She thought about texting back, *I'll just see you later*. She didn't have a whole lot to say to Baby Girl, she was tired and smelly and she just wanted to get through today so it'd be tomorrow, so it'd be the day she would meet up with Travis. But the thought of wasting time in the trailer with her momma wasn't all that alluring, either. In the end she texted Jim, *Don't need a ride, taking the bus home.* At least driving around with Baby Girl would give her something to do.

It was going to rain, Perry could smell it in the air. Baby Girl was slumped down in the driver's seat as Perry walked up, just her forehead visible. She sat up when she saw Perry, shoved something under her seat.

"Was that a bottle?" Perry asked. The car didn't smell like booze, but maybe she hadn't opened it yet.

"No," Baby Girl said. "That was a surprise for later."

The thought of a surprise coming later made Perry feel more tired than ever. Like maybe she should have sent that see-you-later text to Baby Girl after all.

"I'm not up for being out tonight," Perry said. "Ain't you tired?"

"Once we get where we're going, if you want to leave, you can just say so and we'll leave. Okay?"

Baby Girl started the car, put it into reverse. Perry had the feel-

ing that she'd never met her before, this bald person she was letting
drive her somewhere, she looked familiar but Perry had no idea who
she was. She was in the car with a stranger.

"You still mad about last night?" she asked. "About what I told
you?"

Baby Girl laughed, quiet, through her nostrils. "I'm not mad," she
said. "In fact, that's where we're going now. We're going to meet up
with your friend Jamey over by the quarry. He wants to see you."

Perry was wide awake now. "Are you serious? We're going to meet
up with Jamey?"

"Yep," Baby Girl said. "He wanted to meet up with both of us, but
I figured that was just because he knew you wouldn't come alone. So
let's go see him!"

Her voice was bright, as sugary as a kindergarten teacher's. Baby
Girl never talked like that. She'd even dropped the accent she'd been
using for months, that deep gangsta accent she'd been perfecting for
as long as Perry had been thugging with her.

"I don't want to meet up with him," Perry said. "I haven't even
been talking to him. I'm meeting up with Travis tomorrow. *That's*
who I want to meet up with."

"I know you don't," Baby Girl said. "But he's been on our asses.
Fucking with us. Let's go fuck with him. Besides, you might think
he's cute once you see him."

"Did you hear what I said? I don't want to go."

"I told him we'd meet him," Baby Girl said. "I said we'd be
there."

"If you don't stop driving us there I'm going to jump out the next
time you stop," Perry said. She meant it, bracing her body, her fingers
on the door handle.

"Please," Baby Girl said, her voice weak, like her throat was too
wet. She coughed into her hand and her voice sounded stronger
when she said, "I need to show this fucker."

Show this fucker what? Perry almost said. Only she knew. It was clear, now, that Baby Girl *was* hurt, she *was* still mad about what Perry had told her in the cell. But she needed Jamey to see that she wasn't any of those things, that she didn't care about him in that way, that she'd deliver her own best friend to him just to show him how little she cared.

Maybe this wasn't a stranger beside her. Maybe this was the real Baby Girl.

"Okay," Perry said. "We'll go, but you ain't leaving me there alone with him."

"You never know," Baby Girl said. "Maybe you'll want me to leave you alone. Maybe you'll beg for it."

Baby Girl *wanted* her to go off with him, Perry could see now, into his backseat or farther into the woods, wanted her to act the whore. So it wasn't just Jamey she wanted to fuck with, abandon. She wanted to leave Perry behind, too, nice and tidy.

"I won't want that," Perry said. She wanted to reassure Baby Girl almost as much as she wanted to scream at her. A few drops of rain hit the windshield, as fast and hard as rocks. She was being driven to meet up with that fucking weirdo in the rain, all so Baby Girl could prove to herself that she was right about them, that she was right about the world.

"So what's the surprise you got under the seat?" Perry asked. She felt her voice getting away from her, loud and angry. "A box of condoms? You can watch since you seem so interested in us falling in love. I'll show you how it's done."

Baby Girl reached under her seat, brought out a gun. Perry recognized it: Charles's gun, the one Baby Girl kept in a keepsake box under her bed. She held it pointed at Perry's lap, her finger on the trigger.

"Surprise," she said, her voice bright again, like it was a cake and not a gun.

"You look fucking stupid holding that," Perry said. "If you're trying to scare anyone it ain't going to work."

Baby Girl pulled the trigger. *Click.* Perry flinched, her body moving beyond her control. She knew it wasn't loaded, they'd never been able to find any bullets in Charles's room, but it was like her brain was separate from her body, and knowing the gun wasn't loaded didn't matter at all. Her body seized, she couldn't move her arms if she wanted to.

"Oh shit!" Baby Girl said. She shoved the gun back under her seat, laughing. "Look how you jumped, and you even knew it wasn't loaded! Just wait until that fucker sees it. You think he'll shit himself?"

The accent was coming and going now, Baby Girl forcing out her laughter so hard that she was heaving. It took Perry a second to realize she wasn't laughing no more, her heaving wheezes turning into short barks, something she'd never heard from Baby Girl before. She was crying now, her face all wet, the sobs coming out as forced and unwanted as coughs. "Oh shit," she kept saying. "Oh shit, oh shit."

The rain was coming down hard now, the sky dark above them and darker where they were driving to. Perry reached over and flipped on the wipers.

She couldn't even remember the last time she'd talked to Jamey. She didn't give a shit whether he liked her now, didn't care if he wanted her. It had once seemed so important. Perry had never been ugly, not a day in her life. Knew if she wanted to she could have whoever she wanted. Sometimes she even caught herself posing just so for Jim, hoping he'd take in her curves and she'd see in his face that she was right: everyone was a starved animal. Even Baby Girl.

Even herself, she was starting to see. She was as raggedy as the whores in that cell, raw for the power she had over whoever. She was fucking tired. With the windows up the air was too close in Baby Girl's car, she could practically smell the salt from her tears. She was sick of all of it, wanted to wake up in the morning knowing she wouldn't be sneaking out her window for a long time, maybe ever again.

Unless it was to see Travis. The thought of tomorrow, of him, felt like a promise. This rain would eat shit and the sun would come out and she'd kiss Travis again. And she'd have made things right for Baby Girl, made peace between them so they could go their separate ways for a while.

"Okay," Perry said, after Baby Girl had quieted. "Let's go set that fucker straight."

She didn't have any idea what setting him straight meant. Maybe just showing up would be enough. And she didn't know why she had to say anything at all. Baby Girl, through the gun and the tears and everything, had kept driving, and they were already there.

JAMEY SAW THEM DRIVE UP, he'd been watching awhile, watching until the shineless brown of Dayna's car appeared every now and again through a break in the trees, until he could hear the engine, until they had slowed and were pulling onto the short white shoulder and parking. The rain had slowed to a drizzle, but the sky was still dark, and he stood under the umbrella he'd bought on the way over. Black, so he'd look mysterious. But maybe he should have just stood in the rain instead. It was tougher. When it came down to it, though, he just couldn't risk what it might do to his hair, how it might make his clothes cling to his fleshy body.

He felt sick, like he might need to use the bathroom, but that always happened when he was excited. He knew he wasn't an attractive man, but he'd had women before, women nearly as pretty as Perry, and he knew what he had to do to seal the deal.

He'd have to present himself like he knew his flaws, had spent a long time feeling awful about them, but had made a brave kind of peace with them. He'd have to keep his thumb over his cleft, his curled knuckles on his chin, like he was trying to come off a deep thinker, only Perry would probably see that he was actually trying to hide his deformity. Every once in a while he'd have to move that hand up to his hair, run his fingers through, so she'd see that he cared about his appearance. He'd raked a comb through his hair over and over before getting out of his momma's car, to make sure his hand wouldn't get caught on no knots. His other hand he'd have to keep loose at his side. Empty. So she could see he didn't have no designs. So she could see how relaxed he was, how far from making a fist. Only what with the umbrella, he did have something in his fist, but no matter, he couldn't see how she'd have a problem with that. He'd have to have mud splatters on his jeans cuffs, on the tips of his boots, so she could see he was a workingman, a man with a life outside of her. And he'd have to nod at her, say *Hey*, keep his distance, let her come to him. Some girls were huggers, but he didn't figure Perry for one of them, and even if she was, he'd let her put her arms around him, he'd keep his own arms down and wait it out.

If you let a woman know how much you've been looking forward to her presence, you're dead in the water. Might as well be a skunk, might as well be the janitor. He knew what he needed to do, it was only that he was out of practice. It had been years since he'd been free to lure and catch. He hoped it was like riding a bike. He hoped he'd put on just enough cologne, enough to make him smell like a man but not enough to overtake the dirt and sweat he'd worked up. A girl had once told him she'd been afraid when she smelled his sweat. That was the moment she knew she was done for. Her voice a tickle in his ear, her hair wet with her own sweat. There was always a moment when they met halfway: when his own fear had retreated and when hers had swelled. He had to make room for it. It was like he was the woman and she the man, her swollen fear meeting his growing void. For that second, they were equal.

Right now he and Perry were far from that moment, far from being equal. So much work to be done. But sometimes all that work could come about in an afternoon, and he'd been laying a foundation for weeks already. They were getting out of the car now, he could see Dayna's bald head and white T-shirt, he could see Perry's blond ponytail. Neither had an umbrella. The rain was like spittle now, seeming to coat everything, blowing in despite his umbrella and coating his arms, working its way into the cotton of his shirt. His stomach gurgled, something hot surged in his bowels. He had never been face to face with her, but he'd been so with her momma, and he'd been in her room, in her bed. Her underwear was alive in his back pocket, like it had a heartbeat. He felt impatient for her to know him the way he knew her. He raised his thumb to his lip.

Dayna would likely wander off, leave them to it. She was a prideful kind, didn't want to let on how badly she wanted to watch, how badly she wanted to be the one getting lured. He'd only have to worry about her for as long as the small talk lasted.

They were closer now, picking their way down the path. He was midway up the ledge that looked over the quarry, a width of dirt and roots that made a kind of natural bridge, only there wasn't no ropes or rail to hold on to. But you had to be an idiot to get too close to the ledge. He'd given himself a good six feet.

Perry's ponytail swung behind her, her breasts moving ever so slightly with each step, her shirt riding up when she needed to use her arms for balance. Dayna plunged along beside her, her own breasts a sexless shelf, huge and sloppy and heaving. Jamey felt sorry for her. If he was a different man, maybe . . . but he was who he was.

"Hey," he called. He unfurled the knuckles at his chin and waggled his fingers in a kind of wave, but kept his thumb where it was. He worried it looked faggoty, or like something an uncle might do, but neither girl seemed to notice, each focused on just getting down the trail and up to him as quickly as she could. A red truck came down the road, followed soon after by a silver hatchback. Neither slowed near Dayna's car, and if they looked, it was doubtful they could see him up on the ledge, or the girls coming down the trail, especially on a dark day like this. At a glance from a passing car it was just the woods, Jamey knew. You had to slow down, stop even, and be looking for something in order to see anything. The girls were just fifty feet away now. A fart escaped, hot and wet, and Jamey was glad for the open air. He'd never lost control before, he'd always made it to a bathroom with plenty of time. It was something to keep faith in. No use worrying himself into a froth, as his momma liked to say, and having to excuse himself to find a tree or drive off in search of a toilet.

Now they were before him, not ten feet away. "Hey," he said again. Perry's ponytail was all wet, as pointy as a dagger. Dayna's whole head looked dunked, a bib of wet seeping down her shirt. Up close her lips looked wrong, like she meant to draw a clown mouth but forgot to fill it in. He felt that surge of pity for her again. Maybe, if all went right, he could do something for her, too. But first things first.

"Hey," Perry said. "You Jamey?" Her voice sounded lower than he'd expected, like her momma's, only without the scratch of too many lost nights. He'd heard her yelling to Dayna before, he'd heard her calling *Bye-bye* to her momma, but her voice had been higher then, more girlish. Fake. He felt thrilled to be hearing her real voice. He nearly thanked her.

"You're old as *fuck*," Dayna said. "You ain't in high school, you fuckin' liar."

Of course, he'd been expecting that, too. Before, he hadn't had to worry so much about not looking young enough, but the years had passed, and he'd gotten soft and pale in jail, eating clods of meat and greens so wasted they'd turned yellow and puddles of what the line cook called *congealed*: fluorescent jellied desserts with mystery fruit suspended inside them. And the years had passed. Nothing he could do about that. He'd rubbed tinted lotions he found at the drugstore on his face and arms, he'd lifted his momma's jumbo cans of chili above his head and curled them in toward his face, he'd grown out his sideburns and started combing his hair back. Only those ended up being the trends from before he got locked up, and now he just looked like a man reliving his glory days. A man with a cleft lip and a soft belly and stumpy legs. He could name all his flaws for anyone who asked. Draw a map of them for Dayna if need be. But that could wait.

"I got held back," he said through his thumb, aiming his answer at Perry. Better for Dayna to get the picture—no one wanted her here—sooner rather than later. "And I've always looked old for my age. I ain't been carded since I was fourteen years old." He moved his hand up to his hair, raked his fingers through. Shifted his weight to the other foot, so he'd look casual, so he'd look unperturbed by what Dayna had said or what she might say next.

"You get held back a whole decade?" Dayna asked. She smiled, her cartoon mouth in an ugly grin, but her eyes were red, the flesh underneath puffed and veiny. She'd been crying, Jamey realized. All girls, when you got right down to them, were pretty much the same. They all wanted to be the prettiest to someone, they all cried when things got to be too much for them.

"You been crying?" he asked. He tried his best to make his voice sound concerned. "Everything all right?" He knew she wouldn't want him noticing that, wouldn't want to talk about it with him most of all. And he knew it was the perfect thing to get her to shut up, to get her to mumble how she was going for a walk, or how she'd be waiting in the car. Or, even better, how she'd come back for Perry after a while. He was betting on that one, betting her embarrassment would send her somewhere she couldn't see them.

But it was Perry who spoke next. "We just came to let you know we ain't into you," she said. "So you can just go ahead and lose our numbers. Stop waiting around by the computer for us to show up. I got a boyfriend and Baby Girl thinks you're a shithead."

It was clear she hadn't wanted to use the word *shithead*, it wasn't mean enough. Jamey knew the feeling. What was also clear to him was the wavering in her voice. A girl's loyalty to her friend would make her say anything, try anything, Jamey knew.

A boyfriend, for example. That had to be a lie. He hadn't seen her with no boyfriend, hadn't heard Myra mention it, either. Why would she say it? It was a risk on her part. How could she know how he'd react to it? Some guys might be driven off by shit like that. Not him. He felt as old and wise as a tree trunk. One little chop couldn't take him down.

"It's okay," he said. "I ain't into Dayna like that. I never have been." He stopped just short of saying *I'm into you*, wanted to maintain whatever aloofness he had left, but he knew he had to say out loud what they were both wondering: Who was he here for? Had to calm them, reassure Perry most of all. He was her devoted. Another thing his momma said. *Are you my devoted? Huh, are you? Yeah, you are.* Her voice like a dog's tongue on its own butthole. Another hot wave roiled through his bowels.

"Don't say my name," Dayna said. "You don't know me." She sounded like one of those white people who wanted to be black. Plenty of those in the jail, all of them crazy enough to swallow a sharpened toothbrush just so they could shit it into an enemy's eye.

"Anyway," he said, his eyes on Perry. "You want to go somewhere and talk?"

He might even show her the underwear. Why else had he brought it? He needed her to see that he was serious, he'd done his work. Maybe she'd be scared. Even better.

"Did you hear what I said, dummy?" Perry asked. The rain was picking up. Her eyes had slitted themselves against it. Jamey was shocked to realize she was near ugly. He could see the mean parts of her momma in her. Wet wasn't her look.

"Did you hear what *I* said?" he asked. "You ain't got to worry about me and Day—your friend here."

The girls cut eyes at each other, laughed. It irked him, he couldn't help it. This was one aspect of girls being friends that he did not like. Still, he smiled along with them, letting his thumb drop away.

"It ain't no use," Dayna said.

"Nope," said Perry.

Things hadn't gone his way before, plenty of times. Sometimes it took awhile for the girl to warm up to him, trust her emotions. He'd even given up a time or two, walked away empty-handed and disappointed. But he felt like it was too soon to make that kind of a call.

The girls were turning away from him now, still laughing a little. Dayna was shaking her head like he was a lost cause.

"Hey now," he said. "It ain't polite to leave the table before you're excused. I want to talk to you." He could hear how firm he sounded, how adult, but he hoped it came off as macho.

"What do you want to say?" Perry asked, only half-turned back toward him. "Might as well say it now, 'cause I ain't going nowhere with you to hear what it is."

With her body turned that way he could see the beginnings of a roll of flesh at her belt line, just a hint at what was to come if she wasn't careful. Jamey wanted to warn her of it, warn her that she'd get older and her body would get soft and no matter how hard she tried she'd never be young again, never be as young as even one second ago. He wondered did she get lonely for her past yet, did she? Even if it wasn't all that great of a past. Even if it was a hell. It was still a bundle of days gone.

"I like you," he said. Sometimes when it had gone bad he'd had to lay it all out on the table, fan out his cards face up and name them one by one. This felt different. Something about how rusty he was. Something about all those days gone by. Something about Jim, and how much he wanted the man to like him, but also how much he wanted to take a fishing hook to his belly. This time felt more raw. He felt himself get hard, another card.

"And I want to be with you," he went on. It seemed like such a simple thing. He had this difficulty in his pants, this stiff offering, and she only had to take it. Accept it like a birthday gift, only there wasn't even no ribbon to have to unbow. He took a step toward her.

"He's got a fucking *boner*," Dayna said. "Look!"

He only wanted to quiet her down, only wanted Perry to listen to him and not her, only wanted to place a hand on her arm so she could feel that he was a human being, not a monster, not a stranger. A friend. "That's just my pants," he started to say, his touch firm on Dayna's forearm, his own dry hand soaking up the cold and wet of her, and okay, he pushed her a little, nudged her really. Move back, move away from here, you're ruining it, can't you see you're ruining it?

But it was like a shock went through her, a jolt, his hand making her seize up, grunt an unwomanly *unh*, the arm he touched yanked up and away, her other arm going around the back of her and returning with the blackest gun he'd ever seen. With a gun. A gun. He repeated the words to himself, trying to believe his eyes. A gun! A chop of a laugh burst from him, maybe he was hoping it was a joke, maybe he was beyond his own control now. The whole thing felt beyond real. Felt like something he was watching. Next on the reel was Perry's face, her mouth in an open rictus, so it *was* a joke! He reached out his arm again. He had the urge to stick his fingertip in the barrel hole, plug it up, show them he was a good sport.

Dayna lunged toward him, and then he was in the air, as weightless as if he was in the water, windmilling his arms like he was attempting the backstroke. He felt the gun fly off his finger. He tried to locate its arc with his eyes, could only take in the blurred wipe of the walls of the quarry, growing taller and taller, the ledge he'd just been standing on getting farther and farther away from him. He was falling. His underwear filled with the warm liquid of his bowels, finally, every part of him beyond his control now. He thought of his momma, the fallen cakes of her breasts. Whose hand on his pants front, which momma? He knew he'd land soon. His brain allowed one final thought, and it broke his heart before the rocks broke his body: Why so much silence? Why weren't they screaming?

SHE'D PUSHED HIM, hard, letting go of the gun and jamming her hands into his chest, getting ready to charge him if he came back at her, but his boot caught on a root and he tumbled backward. Right off the ledge. He was there and then gone. It wasn't two seconds before she heard him land, a clattering and then a wet thump. He hadn't even yelled. The gun had gone over with him, stuck to his finger. The stupid gun! Baby Girl felt like someone had wiped the spiderwebs from her eyes. Everything seemed bright, the wet trees and the rocks as crisp as if someone had painted them there and then outlined them in black. *A good news morning* is how Charles liked to word it. Only it wasn't the morning and there wasn't no good news.

A clattering and then a wet thump. All because she pushed him. All because she'd pulled the gun. All because she'd brought the gun in the first place. All because of her gaping ache. All because of her bald head, her fleshy belly, her ugly self. He hadn't even yelled. Before she knew it Baby Girl was bent over, upchucking into the dirt. A wiggling pool of bile formed at her feet. She hadn't eaten anything since the day before.

"Is he dead?" The words stung her mouth. She spat. "You think he's dead?" Another gurgling mouthful tumbled forth.

"I don't know," Perry was saying. "I don't know. It's hard to say. He could be alive. He could be."

When Baby Girl felt sure she wouldn't heave again, she straightened, looked at Perry. Only then did she notice it was still raining, Perry's face streaming, her eyes blinking away the water. The rain would wash away the bile. Maybe it could wash away what she'd done. But Perry was right. He could be alive down there. The thought was enough to compel them both to the edge to see for themselves.

He was on his side, his arm flung out like he was reaching for something, his back arched. His legs were together, his feet one on top of the other, as neat as peanut shells, though he'd lost a boot. He'd have looked like he was asleep but for his head, which was facing up, his neck just a rope of jelly now.

There wasn't any blood that she could see, and Baby Girl knew it was probably like someone took a meat mallet to his insides, everything a mush now, blood running wherever, all dams burst but the dam of his skin. That's how it was with Charles, his head like a thick balloon swelling with blood.

She didn't see the gun. "Where did the gun go?" she heard herself ask. She had wanted to say, *We need to do something for him*, but the thing about the gun had come out instead. Her voice as toneless as a bee's whine. *I didn't know!* she wanted to scream. *It's not my fault! How could I know? I take it back! I take it back!* She should push Perry over, too, and then jump in after. Dive headfirst so her brain would go splat.

"Look," Perry said, pointing into the quarry with all the fingers on both hands, like she was frozen that way, like she was about to dip them into a vat of something, or was showing off her nails. Baby Girl looked. The socked foot was pedaling fast. The fingers on his flung arm were fluttering, like he was typing in his sleep.

"He is," Perry said. "He's alive." She sounded fascinated, lured in, like she was narrating her own dream.

"We have to go down there," Baby Girl said. "We have to get

him." When Charles had his accident he'd lain by the side of the road for ten minutes before someone finally stopped to help him. People had come forward later to say they'd seen him but figured someone else had called for help already. But no one had, his brain swelling the whole time. When the paramedics finally arrived his head looked like it was near to popping. In the hospital they'd opened up his skull, stuck tubes in, the blood they drained out as black as ink.

There was a winding, rocky path that could get you to the bottom, and Baby Girl started walking toward it. It was Charles down there, Charles with the pulled taffy neck and the flung arm and the eyes that couldn't look nowhere but up. The thought had her nearly running.

"No," Perry shouted. "Don't."

"You think we should call nine-one-one instead?" Baby Girl asked. She hadn't thought of that until now. She'd just wanted to be down there, holding his ruined head in her hands, calming his pedaling leg as best she could. Like he'd wake up just fine if someone came to see him. Calling 911 seemed like something she'd heard of, not something she could actually do.

"No," Perry said. "I think we should go back to the car and drive home. Get out of this rain. Get out of these clothes."

"We can save him," Baby Girl said.

"He's dead, Dayna."

Perry hadn't said her real name in a long time.

"He's dead, and he was trying to hurt us, and it was self-defense." Perry's hair was coming out of its ponytail, tentacles of wet hair clinging to her face. She looked pale, drowned. Ugly.

Baby Girl looked again. The leg had stopped.

"We can't just leave him down there," Baby Girl said, but she felt herself weakening. What could they do? Drag him up? Then what? She let herself remember him lunging, remember the fear she felt.

Remembered that it was she who'd pushed him. Her fault, self-defense or not.

"We'll go home and decide what to do from there," Perry said. She backed up a couple tentative steps, keeping her eyes on Baby Girl. Turned. Walked toward the car.

Baby Girl followed.

THE TRUTH WAS PERRY WAS ELECTRIC with the horror of what had happened. There Jamey went, over the edge, over and over and over, nothing to be done. She hadn't meant . . . but that was a useless thought. Of course she hadn't meant it. Tons of shit she hadn't meant, but it had all happened anyway.

Another truth: she didn't want to have this with Baby Girl. They were done with each other, it was clear, would have gone their separate ways right as soon as Baby Girl dropped Perry off back at the trailer. Until now. Now they had this secret to share.

And so already Perry was trying to make it something else. Something tidy. He'd wanted to hurt them. He'd fallen, he was probably dead. He was not who he said he was. It was an accident.

She could even feel herself wanting to shout something like *Get over it!* at Baby Girl. Could feel herself actually believing it was nothing to get upset about.

But there was no need to yell, Baby Girl was right behind her, both of them nearly at the car now.

"Where are we going?" Baby Girl asked once they were inside.

"Just drop me home," Perry told her. Her voice came out in a croak.

"I thought we were going to decide what to do."

"We have decided," Perry said. She looked out the window, away from Baby Girl.

"You've decided," Baby Girl said. But she started the car, didn't say nothing more. The wipers clearing the windshield, time already passing.

Perry pulled down the visor to look at herself in the mirror, something she always did when she felt shaken loose, something she had started doing back when she had first had sex, with a man who worked at the same shop her momma did. He was nineteen and Perry a few weeks into being fourteen. She'd watched him whenever she went to visit her momma after school. He had a genuine fang and a tattoo of something sharp peeking below his shirtsleeve. Later she found out it was a quill, *quill*, a word she didn't know until he'd said it. She'd wanted to laugh but hadn't. And he'd watch her, too, black glinty eyes on her while he mopped or stocked the cold case.

It was the first time Perry felt how curiosity could shift, black and churning and alive, into desire.

He'd called in sick one day, which meant Perry's momma had to go in, and he came by the trailer when Perry was home alone from school. "Hey, show me your bedroom" was all he said. They'd done it quickly on the top of her bedcover, him saying "Ready?" at the exact moment he'd pushed into her, the pain as jagged and bright as a small explosion, though there'd barely been any blood. Then again in the shower, which Perry had pretended to enjoy as much as he did, but really it just felt practical, like some kind of a procedure. Easy. And the way he looked at her during. *Bow down*, she nearly said, and she knew he would have.

After he left, Perry looked at her face in her momma's hand mirror. She looked the same as she always had. It was a letdown. Nothing had changed, only everything had.

But when she looked in the mirror now she saw that she was different. Smudge of Myra. Faded and fading. And then she allowed the thought she allowed whenever she felt like she might be disappearing: *Least I ain't Baby Girl.* Bloom of relief. She could get through this, past it. No more than a tick on her timeline. Just had to stay strong till the next tick.

Plus, it hadn't been her who'd pushed him. There was always that: it hadn't been her.

TONIGHT HE'D APOLOGIZE to Herman. Make it clear that he didn't take kindly to being asked about his daughter by a man in prison for taking one alive, leaving her naked and mostly dead in a farmer's hayfield. But Jim knew that if you treated prisoners like animals, they tended to act like exactly that. If you treated them like they were human beings, with real emotions and brains, they'd act the part.

Herman was curled in his cot like always, hands in his armpits, facing the wall. Jim rapped on the cell bars with his nightstick.

"Hey," Jim said, trying to force some kindness into his voice, but still the word landed like an embroidered turd.

Herman uncurled, lay flat on his back. Jim took it as a good sign. He saw that Herman's bandage was smaller now, and it didn't wrap his head. Another good sign.

"Herman, I'd like to apologize for jabbing you in the eye. It wasn't right. I should have explained to you that you don't talk to no one about their kin rather than putting the hurt on you."

The man seemed to be listening, his wild eye moving side to side.

"Okay?" Jim said.

"You didn't let me finish," Herman said. There was a whine in his voice, something no grown man should resort to. It turned Jim's stomach.

"Go on, then," Jim said. "But mind yourself."

"I asked after your daughter for a reason," Herman said. "And it wasn't 'cause I wanted to scare you, or have something to think about at night. I'm a changed man now that I have a personal relationship with Jesus."

A personal relationship. The prison chaplain, a lady with short bushy hair, always talking to the men about becoming buddies with God. Sometimes it worked. Sometimes the men tried it on and took it off like a pair of pants. Jim started to feel impatient.

"Go on, then," he said again.

"One of the men used to be in here knows your daughter. Been talking to her. Working on her. You know what I mean?"

"Perry?" Jim hadn't meant to say her name out loud. Didn't want none of the men knowing it. But there it was. Saying it then felt like a conjuring, like he'd whispered her name right into a demon's ear and then pointed the way.

"I don't know her name," Herman said, rubbing his wild eye till it squished. "All's I know is Jamey been talking to someone he claims is your daughter. Got himself online and found her there."

"Jamey?" Saying that name aloud pricked his heart with fear.

"You remember Jamey," Herman said. "Looked like nothing, said nothing, was nothing?" Herman laughed. "He got out some months ago. Been writing to me now and again. Lives with his momma."

Jim didn't remember a Jamey but knew he could find out who he was easy enough. "Why are you telling me this?" he asked the man. "What are you trying to get in return?"

"Nothing," Herman said. "Jesus Christ told me I gotta dump all the trash, clear the land and start over. I know I got a affliction that's out of my control, so I got to give it to God."

"Jamey," Jim said again. A carousel was starting up in his mind, real slow but gaining speed. Music and lights. Perry as a girl, Perry now, Perry on the computer, a black shadow creeping up behind her.

"Yeah," Herman said. "He was in here 'cause that high school girl stabbed him with his own knife and got away. He told me they found him with his finger in the wound like a stopper, claiming a raccoon got him. And since there wasn't no penetration on his part, excuse me for saying the word *penetration*, it's a trigger word for me that I am to avoid, but anyway since there wasn't none of that he got a kiddie sentence and left here with most of his life still before him. But you need to know he's got intentions on your daughter. *Perry.*"

Now the carousel was deafening, the lights flashing wildly, Jim's heart like a tennis ball against the side of a house. He knew he should feel afraid for her. But all he felt was rage. Stupid, so fucking stupid. A man should look forward to going home. When he got there he'd make her delete her Facebook, change her phone number. Maybe he and Myra would look into a new school for her as well. And he'd find this Jamey and destroy him.

But first he unlocked the cell door, stood over Herman with his nightstick raised. Even in his blindness the man recurled, protecting himself. "Thank you for telling me," Jim said. "If I ever hear you saying her name again, you'll wish for the day I got you in the eye." Jim hit the side of his bed, over and over, at first to scare the man, and later he felt ridiculous for doing it, it seemed like something a bad actor would do in some TV show Myra might watch, but right then it had just felt so good.

A COUPLE ON THEIR WAY to a dark spot on the far side of the quarry, vibrating with desire like two tines of a tuning fork, the condom in the boy's pocket like a brand on his leg, didn't even look down. A stray dog saw but didn't know what to make of it. Barked once, got spooked by its echo, moved on. A boy who'd just made a slingshot, knew where he could get some real mean rocks, asked his daddy later that night did he know there was a mannequin all twisted up at the bottom of the quarry? "Ain't that something," his daddy answered. Cars drove in, parked, couples argued and kissed and swatted at each other. Four airplanes and a helicopter flew over. Then there were days of rain. Days and days. No one went to the quarry, hardly anyone went out long enough to make a difference. When the sun returned so did the boy, something about that mannequin kept occurring to him. (Did mannequins have gray skin sometimes? It niggled at him, a splinter in his brain.) But when he looked down all he saw was a shoe, and he couldn't even be sure it was the same kind of shoe the mannequin wore. Someone had already got the mannequin, the boy decided, took it home to live in the basement or took it to the dump to be tossed in a pile. He felt sad about that, but only for a moment, because then his eye fell on the perfect rock, round but jagged, just heavy enough to sail through the air but still cause some real damage. His mouth watered, thinking of a broken window, a crack in a windshield, or maybe, if he felt mean enough, a bruise. He forgot about the mannequin, never thought about it in his waking moments ever again.

THE DOORBELL RANG, something Myra hadn't heard in ages. No one ever came by, and when they did they knocked or just looked in through the screen door and asked whatever it was they'd come to ask. Or came and sat down on the stoop with her, like Pete had. For a moment Myra thought it might be coming from the television, was *The Price Is Right* on? But no, the TV sat dark. She'd turned it off as a challenge to herself: she'd do something constructive, she'd do anything else aside from watch TV or drink. That had lasted a solid hour, an hour she spent bargaining with herself. Okay, I'll only do *one*. But which one? The beer had won out. It was room temperature, almost flat. It had lived under her and Jim's bed for quite some time.

And then *DING ding DING ding*. Myra saw through the screen door that it was an enormous woman, heaving for breath, wearing a sleeveless housedress, her arms like dough on dough. The woman leaned on a cane that looked like it might snap under her weight, her other hand gripping the rail. Which hand had she used to ring the doorbell? How had she stayed upright?

"Help you?" Myra asked, coming to the door.

"I'm asking have you seen my son," the woman wheezed.

"Your son?" Myra said. "I don't know you or your son."

"His name's Jameson," the woman said. Her chins trembled.

"Don't know him," Myra said.

"He ain't come home," the woman said, and Myra saw that what she had taken for sweat was actually tears. Her whole face was wet, her eyes positively burbling over.

"I'm sorry to hear that," Myra said. "How old?"

"Jamey's thirty-three," the woman said, and Myra nearly laughed.

"Your son's in his thirties? And you wondering where he's at?" As she often did, she felt her throat swell with pride that she didn't baby Perry like some parents babied their children. "He's probably at some girlfriend's house," she said to the woman, "or sleeping off a bender!" She had meant to calm the woman with these possibilities, but she saw that they'd landed wrong, saw fat new tears pushing every which way out the woman's eyes.

"Jamey don't have no girlfriend," the woman said. She let go of the rail to paw at her face, wipe the tears away, but they kept coming. "And he ain't got nowhere else to sleep."

"Well," Myra said, and let it hang there. She wanted this woman to move on, limp over to the next trailer, quit crying helpless and sloppy on her steps. "Well," Myra said again. "You got a picture?"

The woman started, like the thought hadn't occurred to her until just now. "No, I don't have no picture with me." She said the word like *pitcher*.

"Bring me a picture," Myra said. "And I'll take in his face and keep an eye out. I work at the truck stop off the highway, and I see people coming and going all the time. I'll ask around, once I got a picture." She would have offered this woman anything to get her off the porch.

"Mm-hmm," the woman said, nodding, looking past Myra into her trailer. This moment of preoccupation had halted the tears; this was the kind of woman who could handle only one thing at a time.

"He ain't *here*," Myra said, more sharply than she'd intended, but she hated this woman, this wounded whale, this *thing* that was keeping her from her beer.

"All right, then," the woman said. "I'll bring by a pitcher soon as I can find one that's recent."

"You do that," Myra said, and slowly, so it wouldn't feel like an insult, closed the door in the woman's face. Seeing as how *that* was his momma, Myra didn't blame this Jamey for disappearing for a while. Maybe it'd do the woman's heart some good, having to get out and walk around asking after him. Exercise, fresh air, nothing wrong with that. Even thinking about it made Myra feel refreshed. She'd definitely earned this next sip, and the ones after that.

AGAIN, LIKE SHE'D DONE A DOZEN TIMES over the past few days, Baby Girl picked up her phone and dared herself to make the call. There had been no mention of it on the news, nothing in the newspaper, no police showing up at her house, nothing. If she made the call she could pretend she'd come upon it, she could pretend someone had told her about it, or she could tell the truth: *I pushed a man into the quarry. He was trying to attack me and my friend. He's dead.*

And again she decided not to dial. She could hear Charles in the kitchen, could tell by the metallic pings that he was eating cereal out of an old mixing bowl, banging his spoon with each bite. Told herself she'd better get in there before he ate the whole box, she could always call later. He wasn't going to get any less dead.

She had thoughts like these now. *Any less dead.* Like she was some hack comedian. Really she was just scared, and full of hate. Scared of what would happen when he was found, and hate because she got to breathe even after she'd stopped the breath of another.

Had she, though? Every day her memory got more fogged. He reached for the gun, she tried to get the gun back, he fell into the quarry. Had she pushed him, or had he simply fallen due to the force of the struggle? Did that last possibility make her feel better?

No.

Because the fact was they hadn't done anything, not one single thing, to help him. Or to get his body out. Not a thing.

Baby Girl's uncle Dave was always talking about hidden evils in the world. "Evil is everywhere, Dayna," he'd say, mixing creamer into his coffee, or cutting into his chicken tender, or during a commercial. "It could be in the most beautiful woman you ever saw. It could be in your own brother."

I'm evil, Baby Girl had always wanted to say, just to scare him. Only now she wanted to say it to him because it was true. Perry hadn't forced her to drive away, Baby Girl had driven them away herself. She had tried to argue, but she hadn't tried hard enough, and in the end it was a relief to go along with Perry, to pretend they'd call someone or do something only so they could get in the car, lock the doors, and drive away.

It still felt like a relief, days later. And that shamed her.

"I ate it all," Charles said, before Baby Girl could even ask him if he had. "And now I have to poop." He had already forgiven her for hitting him, as she hoped he would. The events in his life now were like commercials he'd watched, not all that real.

"Make sure you close the door," Baby Girl said.

"Of course!" This was his new phrase, something he'd likely seen on television. Everything was *Of course!*

Baby Girl set to cleaning up his mess. As she passed the microwave she caught a glimpse of her profile in its glass door: round, bald head, second chin unfurling under her jaw. If she saw herself walking down the street she'd feel pity. Why had she done this to herself? What was the point? *It could be in the most beautiful woman you ever saw.* Or the ugliest. She looked like a demon. Before what happened with Jamey the thought would have pleased her. Now she felt wild, like she wanted to hit something. She closed her eyes, saw Jamey go over the edge. Charles grunted in the bathroom; he'd left the door open. *Fucking no-brain is the one who should be dead*, she thought before she could stop herself. Demon.

When Dave got home she'd ask about his church. If she was brave she'd ask after an exorcism, ask to be whipped or burned at the stake or whatever shit they did to people like her.

If she was brave she'd make the call.

Instead she sent a text to him: *I'm sorry.*

PERRY WAS ON THE BUS, on her way to see Travis. It was nice to sit in silence, and even nicer when it was mostly empty and someone had cracked a window and the breeze was coming in all soft and fragrant, only a hint of exhaust every now and again. After Baby Girl had dropped her off, she'd walked to the Denny's, right in the door and straight through to the back, walked right up to Travis and mashed her body against his until he put his arms around her. "All right now," he said, and she realized she was crying, actually crying, the tears hot and wet like tears were supposed to be.

Even now, she wasn't sure why she had cried. She hadn't pushed Jamey. But he had gone over. She just kept seeing his feet, how calm they looked, one on top of the other like he was asleep, only asleep.

And Travis had held on to her until she let go. They sat in a corner booth drinking hot tea, something she'd only ever seen her dumpy English teacher do, even on the hottest days, but with Travis it felt different, felt adult. She had oversugared hers, so she sipped it in a way she hoped looked like she was savoring it, not nearly gagging on it. She and Travis had allowed their thighs to touch, sitting there side by side, but that was all. Then the cook came from the back and said, "These dishes ain't gonna do themselves," said it in a voice like he was noticing the weather, only loudly, and Perry had walked home. They had made plans to meet up again, Travis telling her he'd be off, his mom working, just like he had that day in the hall. Felt like years ago. And now here she was, on her way.

The fact was she was grateful to him. He seemed to like her despite the fact that she had become ugly, it was plain to see anytime she caught a glimpse of herself in the mirror, which wasn't often these days if she could help it. She looked like she did whenever she got rained on. She would always look rained on, she knew. It made her feel powerless, like she'd lost a weapon she didn't even know she had. She had wilted, something Myra always warned her about, and she had let Jim think losing her Facebook and changing her phone number was the reason.

She hadn't been the one to push him. She waited for the police to show up at the trailer so she could tell them. *It wasn't me.* But they hadn't so far, and there hadn't been anything about it in any of the news programs Myra watched. Perry liked to think Jamey had gotten up and walked away, was hiding out, cursing himself for letting two bitches get the best of him. She was half scared he'd show up to push her over something. But, those feet. No way he had walked anywhere.

If she had a car she might have driven out there herself. Taken a look. And maybe Baby Girl already had, how could she know?

She was nothing special now, just an old dirty sheet. *But even old dirty sheets need a bed*, she thought to herself, that old wickedness like a tingle in her gut. Maybe being in Travis's would make her new again, turn her into something else.

A foul smell was coming in from the window. Perry knew it was likely the piles of manure for sale outside the hardware store they were passing, but still she couldn't shake the feeling that the smell was her.

NOW IT WAS JIM who was calling in, letting his voice weaken and working a catch into his throat, apologizing earnestly but not too many times, which would have been a sure giveaway. Myra never learned that lesson. *I'm sorry, I'm so sorry, hope you can forgive me for putting you out like this*; whoever was on the other end of the line surely rolling their eyes.

Jim simply said, "I hate to do this, but I'm not going to make it in tonight, I'm in bed with the flu or something. Sorry, man."

Cut and dry, that was the key, because a truly sick person wouldn't feel guilty for not coming in. Myra's guilt was as obvious as a burning flag. Myra was all tells.

He found himself doing this more lately. Comparing himself with Myra to see who came out the better person. He always won, and the feeling he got from this had become like an addiction. He had a taste for it, especially on the drive home, when he knew he'd have to pretend not to see so many things. Beer cans and bottles under the couch, Myra in the same shirt as yesterday, the phone off the hook, the TV as loud as a field of blenders. I *don't hide my beer*, he'd think. Or, I've *never been so sick that I don't want a fresh shirt*.

It was what kept them together, now. In the beginning it had been sex and the mystery that comes with slowly realizing you were sharing your time with another human being, same as you, someone that also chewed food and had nightmares and shat in the toilet. It had been a comfort that was hard-won and therefore protected fiercely, and then it had slowly crumbled, fight by fight, into the ruins it was now. Here, in this pile, the week they hadn't spoken to each other because Jim had gotten off the couch and walked into the bathroom in the middle of Myra, hands to her face, crying about being a drunk, the evening's third beer held between her thighs. Over in that pile, all the disagreements over Perry. Gravel shrine to all the nights they'd rejected each other, or worse, done the deed and felt all the lonelier after. Fallen column from when she said she touched that boy. Pebbles and rocks and boulders and whole cracked walls, all overtaking the trailer, and pretty soon it wouldn't be so easy to push everything to the side to make a clear path to the door. They'd just slowly bury themselves alive, one trying to spite the other.

The thing was, he had known this about Myra. Hell, on their first date he'd pushed her up against the wall outside the restaurant and kissed her, had tasted the stale yeast of beer even though she'd been sipping wine at the table. He'd known just what he was signing up for when he married her. And that kept him right where he was more than anything.

"You ain't going in?" she asked him now.

"No," he answered.

"You really sick?" She put her hand to his forehead, and he let her.

"No," he said. "I just need a night off."

This was the truth. Ever since the night he'd beaten Herman's bed to shit, even being in the trailer with his half-drunk wife was more appealing than going into that place. But more than that, he wanted to keep an eye on Perry. She'd been too accommodating when he made her delete her Facebook profile; it had seemed almost like a relief. He'd driven her to and from school each day, and she'd stayed in her room over the weekend, door cracked so he could see her in there. Made him wonder if this Jamey was stalking her, if she needed help more than she was letting on. Jim had waffled on going in or calling in, but Perry hadn't come home yet, and that had made his choice all the easier.

"Might take a drive," he told Myra. He hadn't told her about what Herman had said. He didn't want her to get hysterical, and he didn't want to get upset if she *didn't* become hysterical. When he'd insisted Perry get rid of Facebook and change her phone number, he hadn't given Myra a reason, and she hadn't asked. That was how she lived life: dipping her toe in whenever it suited her, and it usually didn't.

Here he went again, comparing. Well, so be it. Myra didn't give a shit, but he did.

And then the doorbell rang. Something in Jim wanted to grab Myra and throw her back on the couch, bark at her to leave it be. Maybe it was because she made sure to swig back the rest of the bottle she was nursing before she heaved herself up. Maybe it was something else, something beyond what he could see.

"It's that woman again," Myra said.

"Which?"

"I never told you," she said, standing over him, her voice flat. "This woman from a few doors over come by asking after her son. Said he ain't been home in days. Thirty years old or something! I told her he's a grown man, he'll turn up if he wants to."

He stood, and now he did push her, just a little, with his forearm, more like he was guiding her back to the couch a hair too roughly. It felt good, great even, but it was a notch on the other side of the tally: now she had one over on him.

"'Scuse," he said, to make up for it. "I'll get it."

"Free country," Myra said.

The woman was enormous, especially on the bottom. Shaped like a chocolate kiss, everything tapering toward the top. Her hair was thin, not nearly enough of it to be proportionate to the rest of her. Jim could smell the baby powder over something sour, and he was touched, she was trying not to be so monstrous. Still, the powder caught in his throat, and when he tried to get out "Help you?" he coughed in her face instead.

"The lady of the house told me if I come by with a photo of my son she'd help spread the word," she said. The flesh on her upper arms trembled; it was clear holding herself up took a considerable amount of effort. "It's been going on six days now that he's been missing."

"You file a report?" Jim asked. He wanted to help this woman. He stood up straight, preparing to answer whatever she said next with *I happen to be in law enforcement.*

"Well, I ain't of the mind to do that since he's been in trouble with the law priorly," the woman said, her arms trembling faster now.

"Oh?" Jim said.

"I ain't proud of it, and he wasn't neither," she said, "but it is what it is. My fear is that he's fallen into old ways, and I'd rather handle that myself than turn him over."

"You say you brought a photo?" Jim asked. He wanted to get a good look at this boy. If he was out breaking the law Jim wanted to be sure he knew what he looked like so he could bring him in himself.

"Yessir," the woman said. She held out a crumpled Polaroid of a young man holding his hand up, mid-yell. An eye and a cheek and part of his hairline, that's all Jim could make out. Even with that little bit, a curl of recognition began unfolding in his gut.

"His name's Jameson. Jamey," the woman told him.

But she hadn't needed to say it, because all at once it came to him. His cell was always meticulous. Another man had tried stabbing him with a fork, and neither could say why. He had called Jim *sir.* He was in prison for statutory rape and assault with a deadly weapon. He had tried to kill a girl, but she had gotten away after stabbing him, leaping a fence and rushing in the sliding glass door of an elderly couple's home, stark naked but for one sock, gash like a wide mouth in her neck, grinning blood.

And his name was Jamey. And he lived just doors away. And Perry hadn't come home when she said she would.

"Jamey, that's right," Myra called out behind him.

Jim hated her, it was a fact that he knew should have shocked him but instead landed as flat and quiet as a feather. Hated her for stopping short when it got too hard, like how she was too lazy a mother to know her daughter was in real trouble. Hated her all the more for the fact that he'd loved her, had once loved to watch her sleep, back when he didn't know she couldn't fall to sleep without a drink in her. *Be that Myra again*, he felt himself think, and then realized that was the same as wishing to be blind.

The woman still held the photo out, her arm trembling, either because she was scared or because she'd never had to hold her arm out for that long. "I've got the day off," Jim told her, "and I'll leave right now and drive around and look for your boy. I've got some ideas. You just go back and wait till you hear from me."

He shut the door before she could ask him how or why or what, and he'd had to put a firm hand on her arm in order to get her to move back so it could close. There was no tautness to her skin, it was all give. Her insides had taken over, this raw meat of a woman, and for a moment he felt bad for Jamey that he had to live with such a creature.

"Why'd you tell that woman you'd do that?" Myra asked him.

But his moment of sympathy had passed. He watched out the window until Jamey's mother had gone back inside her trailer, then he left without answering Myra, left without even pulling the screen door shut behind him.

PERRY SWITCHED BUSES, got off, and walked five blocks. Travis lived in a house amid a clump of other houses. A bona fide *subdivision*, a word she always thought meant "fancy," but people had toys and tires and old bikes and old men in lawn chairs in their yards just as much as they did in the trailer park. Travis's house was white with red trim and no shit in the yard, but no flowers either. Just scorched-looking grass and a gravel driveway, no car parked there, which she hoped meant they could be alone. *I'm going to have sex with him*, she thought to herself as she walked up to his door. She always said it to herself just before, partly to shock and partly because she couldn't believe it, not truly, not until it was actually happening. She tried to picture it: the weight of him, shirt on or off? Off. His hot mouth and cold fingertips, it was always that way. Their feet tangled . . . feet, Jamey's feet.

She was having a hard time getting truly excited. *I'm going to have sex with him*. It wasn't doing the trick. The feet, the fall, always there at the edge of her vision. She was at his door now, staring at her distorted reflection in the brass door knocker, and she reached out to herself, knocked three times.

And then there he was. Easy as that, always so easy, she had to remember. Wearing a white T-shirt and gym shorts, his calves tanned and hairy. And he was barefoot, which thrilled her despite herself, it made it seem like they were familiar that way.

He squinted one eye closed, the hallway dark behind him, the sun at Perry's back. "Hi," he said.

"I'm going to have sex with you," Perry said. The words came so easily, like ice cubes tumbling into a glass.

He pulled the door open, stepped aside to let her in. "Do you want something to drink?" he asked. She wondered if he hadn't heard her, if she'd even said it out loud after all. He had closed the door behind her, both of them in the dark hallway now, and as Perry's eyes adjusted she could see that Travis's mom was the type to fill the walls of her home, as Myra would be if she could nail anything to that wood paneling in the trailer. On the wall nearest her there were a dozen framed photos, each photo holding at least five people, as if Travis's mother needed even her family photos to be filled up. Behind Travis were shelves holding tiny glass figurines, some identical to ones Myra had. Was every adult obsessed with these things that couldn't be touched or handled or loved in any physical way? Maybe this was her attraction to Travis, maybe this was why they understood each other. Their mothers were nurturers of dumb shit. As Travis led the way into the kitchen she took a tiny glass dolphin and put it in her pocket.

In the kitchen the refrigerator held curled drawings, more photos, a years-old calendar from Jiffy Lube, an assortment of magnetic pens. Perry wanted the tiny calendar but left it where it was, and felt a weird pride in it.

"All we have is orange juice," Travis said. "Or I guess water."

"Hey, show me your bedroom," Perry said.

"I don't want to," Travis said, quickly, like he'd had it in his head and was just waiting for his cue.

"Is it dirty or something?"

"No. Well, yeah, it is, but that's not why I don't want to show you. Let's just watch TV or something instead." His voice was cheerful, too bright, like he was forcing himself to stay calm.

There was that weird pride again, that feeling like she was maturing, doing something adult. "It's okay if you're a virgin," Perry said. "It's not a big deal, trust me. I'll tell you what to do." She had never had to beg like this.

"I'm not a virgin," he said quietly, and Perry knew it was true. He wasn't a virgin, and he didn't care that his room was dirty, he just didn't want her to be in there. She'd never cared all that much when people at school called her a slut, she'd always been able to get what she wanted anyway, but maybe Travis did care. In his work uniform he seemed so much like an adult, so beyond high school, but here in his gym shorts and bare feet it was clear he was just a kid, they were both just kids, and he didn't want to be another notch on her belt, or whatever that saying was Myra always used.

But why let her in, then? Why not just shut the door in her face? Why kiss her back at the Denny's, why agree to let her come over today? And then it came to her. He felt sorry for her. Felt sorry for the poor trailer park slut with the ugly friend. He probably thought she'd feel thankful toward him for letting her in despite what she was. Was probably waiting for her to thank him for allowing her her dignity. Instead she reached behind and up her shirt, undid her bra one-handed, watched him watching her breasts release and fall. By now she knew how to take off her shirt and her bra all at once, and she did it now, letting them fall into a twisted clump by her feet.

"Come here," she said, but he already was, bending to pick up her clothes, holding them up against her front, looking down at his feet. He had a black toenail; Perry had seen it when he'd first come to the door, and in her experience that meant he was physical, had dropped something heavy on it, meant he was a man. "No," she said, and pushed her clothes back to the floor.

"No," he said back to her, and tried to bend again for her clothes, but she was quick, she had her mouth on his and her body pressed against him before he could stop her. And he was kissing her back, there was no doubt, he was holding her to him and his fingertips weren't even cold, and it was then that Perry felt the tears in her throat, felt how she'd almost died a little when it seemed like he was going to turn her away, felt how maybe she loved him, maybe she deserved love despite what had happened with Jamey, despite everything that had happened, despite herself.

"Please," he was saying, and Perry answering him, "Yes, of course, yes," only his hands were pushing instead of holding now. "Please stop," he was saying, pulling away from her, backing up until his back was against the refrigerator, a magnet dropping to the floor.

Perry felt that death coming back, a blackness spreading, felt the cold air-conditioning against her skin, the taste of him still on her mouth; he'd eaten potato chips right before she'd arrived. His mom's endless piles of shit, the bowls of potpourri, the cheap framed prints of sunsets and babies in hats, one wall covered in decorative plates, all of it closing in on her like a burial. Now she was the one being pushed over. Had Jamey believed there was a chance with her, as she'd believed with Travis? And then she was on him again, pushing so hard she felt sure she'd split her own lip on his mouth, this time she wouldn't let him up for air, wouldn't give him time to think. She was beautiful, or at least she had been, and that was enough. She wanted him, and more than that she needed him, his kindness and strong hands and how fucking *normal* he was, and when it was over, when he was inside her, he'd feel it, and he'd thank her.

She pushed him to the floor, pulled his shorts down and her skirt up, yanked the crotch of her underwear over, easy as that, she'd have spat into her hand as so many of the other boys had done if she wasn't so worried that it'd mean she'd have to stop kissing him and break the spell. Instead she pushed down until it was done, the pain not unlike the first time. Only then did she pull away so she could look into his eyes, something she'd been looking forward to doing, looking into his eyes while he was inside her, so he could see how much she loved him, could see the endlessness in her eyes.

At first his sadness seemed like an exhausted form of lust, and Perry felt herself give then, it didn't usually happen so quickly for her, but then she saw that it was actual sadness. Sadness and fear as she quaked against him.

"I didn't," he began to say, and Perry felt him come inside her, and she thrust down to take it all in; this was involuntary, she'd have never allowed it, didn't he see how much he meant to her?

When he finished he put his forehead on her shoulder, and she ran her fingers through his hair. It felt good to soothe someone in this way, in the way she herself needed to be soothed. "You see?" she whispered into his ear. "You see how much I like you?"

He lifted his head, to kiss her, she thought, but when she leaned in to receive him, he yanked his head back so hard that it hit the refrigerator, sent a photo of a woman in a lumpy swimsuit fluttering to the floor.

"I didn't want this," he said, his eyes closed, his head still tilted back. "I liked you." He pushed at her until she let him go, her feet hitting the kitchen tile with a hard slap. She could feel the liquid mess they'd made running down her legs, wanted to ask him for a Kleenex or a towel just as much as she also wanted to squeeze her legs together, hold it there for a little longer. She saw in his eyes that either option would only make her look more pathetic to him.

"I want to be your girlfriend," Perry said. She felt wild with wanting to make him understand how she felt, but the words came out in a whine. *Little bitch*, Baby Girl would have said.

"You need to go," he said. "You need to get out."

"You liked me," Perry said, and it came out like a threat. She felt strangled, like her voice would never be the same. She tried again. "You liked me, right? Ain't this what people do when they like each other?"

Travis shook his head. He hadn't pulled his shorts up yet, and she took that as a good sign. She decided right then that she'd do what she swore she'd never do, what she had no interest in doing normally. She got on her knees.

His thing was limp and already dry, soft as a marshmallow in her hand. Perry gathered the spit in her mouth, licked her lips.

"Stop it," he said, and held her wrist until she let go. Pulled up his shorts. "Go home," he said. "Please," he added, and it was that *please* that did it, Perry saw now how wrong she'd been, he was the type to want to cuddle and talk and hold hands and when it was time to do it, there'd be candles and music and a bed, and not the cold, hard refrigerator door at his back, not this attack from a girl he liked but didn't love. She'd been wrong about him, but he'd been wrong about her. For a moment Perry mourned that other girl, that girl he thought she was. Still on her knees, she grieved that she wasn't the type to go to a movie with a boy and not burrow her hand behind his zipper as soon as the lights went down. Grieved that Travis wouldn't save her from herself, or at least distract her for a while.

But then the moment passed. The tile was hurting her knees, she was still naked from the waist up, she was still leaking, there was probably a small puddle on the tile underneath her. They'd fucked, it felt good to think of it in this way, *fucked* instead of *made love* or *done it*, and now he was kicking her out. She would have told him about Jamey, she realized now. She had *wanted* to tell him. Her grief turned over to rage, like a key turning in a lock.

He was standing in the doorway now, waiting for her to get dressed, get up, get out. She did get dressed, so quickly that she put her bra on inside out, but first she took the dish towel hanging off the oven handle, wiped herself, and hung it back up. How easy it was to do mean things, to downright bask in them, though Travis didn't even try to stop her.

When he opened the front door, the bright afternoon made them both squint, and Perry could only make out his mouth when she turned and said, "Don't tell no one about this," and he answered, "There's nothing to tell." She had meant to hurt him, to make it seem like she was the one with regrets, but his quick answer showed her how backward she had it. "Little bitch," she added, but he was already closing the door.

The neighborhood was stone quiet, like everyone had gone inside to take a nap. A hot breeze came and went as she walked to the bus, delivering the smell of her body to her nose. That sour salt smell of sex. She was a walking trash heap of smells now. Ugly and foul. She thought how she'd believed Travis would be her boyfriend. How they'd drive around, go swimming together, how he'd maybe bring fried chicken over to the trailer and help her arrange it on Myra's good platter, how he'd look away like it was nothing when Myra popped the tab on another beer. She felt like laughing, so she did laugh, right there on the sidewalk in front of a house with cracked green shutters. Laughed like those women in the cell had laughed, like they were trying to drown each other out. If she could take it all back she'd have just gone ahead and fucked Jamey, too. It was all the same when you got right down to it. A little bit of her would die, but at least all of him would be alive, she thought, instead of dead and broken at the bottom of her gut. At the bottom of the quarry, she corrected herself.

THE DOORBELL WAS RINGING AGAIN, and because Myra had never shut the door after Jim left, she could see through the screen that it was that woman, that mother from a few trailers over, though she'd changed into a shirt and pants in the hour since she'd last been by.

Myra pushed open the screen door, too quickly it seemed, because the woman jumped when it banged against the stair railing. Sometimes beer could sharpen Myra's senses, make her overenunciate, hear every tiny sound, or go too far when trying to do something physical, like just now with the door. Like everything she did had to mean it.

"You changed," Myra said, in a kind tone, hoping that'd make up for the banged door, and that they could talk about the heat, or fashion, or any goddamn thing aside from her missing son, even for a few seconds. The woman was wearing a shirt with hot-air balloons embroidered in a diagonal across her big middle and melon-colored sweatpants. Something a toddler would wear.

The woman looked down at her balloons, brushed her free hand down as if to clear crumbs. "Yes, I put on outdoor clothing, since I mean to ask you could you drive me around. I can pay you," the woman said, and Myra saw now that she was holding a coffee can half filled with pennies. "I don't know no one else," the woman added, and the apology in her voice showed Myra that she knew what a burden she was, knew it wasn't a normal thing to ask.

Myra knew what it was to be a burden, those days when she couldn't even get up to pour a glass of juice for herself. It almost made Myra feel tender toward her. And sometimes she could convince herself that doing nice things for others was like an atonement, like the preachers on the radio were always talking about. An atonement that could erase a lot of her sins, make room for more. Plus she knew that Jim might see her a little differently if she helped this beast of a woman—not selfish, not drunken. Human.

"I've had a couple," she said. "But if you want to wait a bit while I get some water in me, I could drive you around a little, sure I can. Come on in." She stepped back to give the woman the full width of the doorway, though it was clear she'd have to turn sideways to get in, and in fact she did just that, bumping the coffee can on the door frame, ignoring the pennies that scattered down the steps and into the dirt. Myra took the can from her, set it on top of the television. Not because she was taking it as payment, but because she didn't want no more pennies tumbling out, dotting her rug like flat, dead eyes.

"Make yourself comfortable," she told the woman, who was already huffing her way over to the couch, using her cane as a kind of stake to steady herself as she half-spun into a landing, her feet going up in front of her as she sat. Myra sat in the chair opposite, her back straight, hands folded in her lap. This felt more like a business transaction than a visit.

"You're a godly woman," the woman said to Myra. "This means the world to me." Her cheeks were flushed pink, it was spreading down her neck. Myra knew that feeling well, too. Never could get cool enough, it seemed.

"Oh, I'm just being neighborly," Myra said. She could see now that the woman was flushed partly because she was allowing the tears to come again, that she was quick to cry, that crying was likely an important part of her day. "Get you something to drink? Or a Kleenex?" she asked.

The woman waved her away. "It just overcomes me sometimes." She smeared both palms down her cheeks, wiped them on her pants. "My name is Lulu," she said, "in case I didn't say so before."

"What a lovely name," Myra said, though she was thinking about how years ago she'd taken Perry to see Lulu the killer whale when they'd visited her cousin in Orlando, and she wanted to laugh about this coincidence with someone, but who? Jim would find it mean. Perry would say the whale's name was actually Leelu or some shit. She'd have to save it for one of her regulars at the truck stop. It was something she might even have told Pete. But thinking of him made her shudder.

"And I'm Myra," she said.

"Mm-hmm," Lulu said, as though Myra's name wasn't all that important or believable.

"So just where do you want to drive to?" Myra said, deciding to keep it all business. She remembered she was supposed to be drinking water, and walked over to the kitchen.

"I don't know," the woman said, loudly, as if Myra had walked outside rather than just into the next room. "I ain't left the trailer park in years."

"Is that so?" Myra asked, though she wasn't shocked or even all that interested. She had seen a talk show once where they piped in video of a man who weighed seven hundred pounds, who was stranded in his bed, waiting for the talk show people to cut a hole in his wall and forklift him out of there. At least Lulu was mobile. And in fact it seemed kind of nice, never leaving your home ever again. Never having to go through the motions, pretend you wanted something more in life, when really all you needed was the bed, your home, something cold to drink. Myra held a glass under the tap. Did she really feel that way? Yes, she did. She gulped the water down in three long pulls. She never did like the taste of water, that was one part of the problem.

"Mm-hmm," the woman answered, and now Myra was beginning to understand that this answer was a kind of tic, like how people said *God bless you* instead of *Thank you* sometimes. "Once my boy had his troubles with the law, I got to where I felt embarrassed to be seen out, and I got everything I need right at home. Used to have a boy bring by my groceries on the back of his bike until Jamey got out and came home." The woman mashed her palms down her face again, another tic.

"Well," Myra said, filling her glass back up. "I guess we can go by the truck stop where I work at, then over to the mall off the interstate, and then we can check his favorite bar, if you know where that is?"

Lulu shook her head. "He don't tell me much," she said.

"Well, we'll just do our best, then," Myra said, downing the glass, forcing each gulp down. This drive would be a waste of time, she knew. She would devote no more than forty-five minutes to it. She put the glass in the sink, grateful not to be beholden to it any longer, and trudged back to her chair. She and Lulu looked around, quietly taking everything in. Lulu seeing everything for the first time, Myra trying to see something she hadn't already seen a hundred million times before. The water began its work. "Excuse me," she said, and took herself to the bathroom.

In the mirror she saw how flattened she looked, not sharpened by the beer at all. Flat hair flat eyes flat face flat flat flat. She ran a fingertip around her lips, an old trick she'd do on dates, draw the man's eyes where you wanted him to look. But they had become wrinkled, lost all their fullness, flat like everything else. She was lucky to have Jim, lucky he'd stuck around, she wasn't no prize, not anymore. She felt wistful for him, suddenly. When he returned she'd . . . what? Too many things she had promised to do or be. When he returned she'd just give him a break, that's what. Behave herself. Do right for as long as she could stand it.

When she came back from the bathroom Lulu was holding one of Myra's vintage jars in her hand, holding it up to the light, turning it this way and that. How she'd been able to twist and reach where they sat on the windowsill behind the couch was a mystery. This woman was more able than she liked to let on was what Myra was beginning to think.

"That's a 1929 Mason—" she began to say, wanting to take it from this woman's hands and put it back where it belonged, but Lulu had cut in.

"Your husband truly out looking for him?" Her eyes suspicious, taking Myra in. Myra took the jar from her, it required a bit of wresting, but Myra wasn't about to give in.

"I guess so," she said, and now she did sit next to the woman, it was her goddamn couch after all. "He left right after you did and I ain't heard from him since." Challenging Lulu to say otherwise, to doubt her Jim. She nearly told the woman Jim was in law enforcement, but didn't when she remembered Lulu hadn't wanted to call the cops in the first place. The last thing she needed was for this woman to lose her shit on her couch.

"So that's a good thing," she continued. "He's out looking, and we'll look too." She and the woman stared at each other; neither wanting to be the one to look away. Damned if it would be Myra.

"He's a godly man," Lulu finally said, though it was clear this was yet another tic, something she said when she wanted to seem polite, harmless. Again Myra felt for the woman's son. What a piece of work this thing was.

"Mm-hmm," Myra answered.

"Oh," the woman said, pulling something out of the tiny pocket on the front of her shirt. "Here's that pitcher." She held out a crinkled Polaroid. "So you know who we're looking for."

Myra took it from her, warm and slick with the woman's hand sweat, barely glancing at it at first, merely wanting to go through the motions, but the man in it caught her eye, the picture coming alive, this blurred, furious attempt at capturing a man who didn't want to be captured. This man who turned out to be her Pete, there he was in the same *Ain't skeered* shirt he'd worn that first night, she knew it was him even though she couldn't see his whole face. She heard her own blood in her ears, her vision seemed to go dark at the edges. What in the hell was going on here, exactly?

"You said your boy's name is Jamey?" Myra said, and her words sounded hollow, like echoes, like they were being spoken by someone across a big wide ravine.

"That's right."

"He ain't got a brother, like a twin?" Myra asked, her heart thudding like a drunken giant. She already knew the answer.

"Not that I know of," the woman said, and laughed, a nervous loud giggle that made Myra jump.

"I seen your boy," she said, before she could stop herself. She stood now, backing away, giving herself some room. "I seen him in my very living room not a week ago, only he called himself Pete."

"You?" the woman said, like it couldn't be believed.

"Yeah, me," Myra said.

"You got a daughter?"

Myra searched the woman's face. Her bulging eyes, the thin lashes, the juddering open mouth. "Why you asking me that?"

"It's just they told me he only ever used that name with the young girls he got into trouble with," the woman said, leaning up on her cane; it was clear she was trying to stand.

And then it clicked. The boy in the hat on Perry's Facebook, that boy's name was Jamey. It wasn't her comforts Pete was looking for, Myra saw now. He had a taste for something different. No wonder he asked after her all the time.

"He was here," Myra said. She needed this woman to believe her, to see that she held his interest, *her*, *Myra*, though it only made her feel worse, the beer like a churning river in her belly. "He was here a couple times. He came by the truck stop. He kept me company."

Now the woman was standing. "What you done with my boy?" she was asking, louder and louder. "What? Huh?" She swept an arm near the pictures of Perry. Baby Perry, Perry in second grade, Perry in braces. "You got a daughter, he try something with her, and now my boy's laying dead or dying somewhere 'cause of his affliction?"

"I don't know where your boy is," Myra said. The woman's hysteria was like a balm to her soul; she felt as calm as a corpse. In the face of other people's emotions she often found herself thinking more clearly than ever. So many clues, so many bits of obviousness she had let pass her right on by. "I truly don't."

"You smell like a liquor closet," the woman said, holding up her cane to point it at Myra. "You're nothing but a nasty drunk *ungodly* woman."

And where *was* Perry? Was she missing? How long before it meant she was missing? Was she at the bottom of a ravine somewhere? Myra wanted this woman out, away, this woman with the fucked-up son. She had a beautiful daughter who was meant for something. She was nothing like this woman. Was she? Where was Perry? The woman began yelling, but it was like someone had popped Myra's eardrums. Nothing sounded right. Myra forced herself to tune back in. Focus. Breathe. Get this woman out, find Perry.

"He served his time!" Lulu was screaming. "He served his time!" It was enough to shake Myra, to fully wake her from the ravine. She stood, grabbed the woman's cane, and threw it out the screen door.

"Go get it," she told the woman, and it was true that the woman barely needed it, how quickly she shuffled to the door and down the steps. Took her three tries bending for it before she could get ahold of it. Myra shut both doors, walked into the kitchen for her phone, walked to the couch, walked into the bedroom for her shoes, walked back out to the couch. She didn't know where to begin. Jim would know. She needed to do something. She needed Jim, goddammit. Finally she went back into the kitchen, poured her bottle out, and all the bottles she could find after that. Myra would be damned if she'd go around with a crutch like that dying whale did. She'd be damned if she'd let the world smell it on her for one more second. And it was something for her hands to do while she waited. Perry would be happy to see it when she came home.

NOW BABY GIRL WAS REGRETTING THE TEXT. If they found him, they'd find his phone, and even if it was smashed to bits or drowned in rainwater, they'd know to check and see who was texting him. And it'd lead them to her. She'd meant it, she'd never been more sorry, even after Charles had his accident. But she was fucked.

Dave was in the kitchen making dinner, and by the smell of it they were having microwave pizza rolls again, Charles's favorite. She should have told Dave about the cereal, but even if she had, wild horses wouldn't hold Charles back from eating dinner along with them. She could go in and ask Dave to pray for her. Pray with her. But it had always been a little embarrassing, watching Dave pray. *Lord Jesus*, he always began, and then his voice would catch, like he could cry but was gathering all his strength not to. By the end his hands would be raised up, and once when she was high she'd laughed over the prayer he was saying because he had his hands up so long that it looked like someone had pressed pause while he was raising the roof. She wanted to ask for Dave's help, wanted to believe what he believed, but she knew she'd be faking.

Charles was in his bedroom, sitting at his desk. Sometimes he sat there to draw or write, though forming letters wasn't all that easy for him. Today he just seemed to be staring at the wall in front of him. Back in the day, Baby Girl could go to Charles for anything. He had been the one to buy tampons for her the first time she got her period. He had been the one to tell her never to throw the first punch but never to walk away from one either. That Charles would know what to do.

"Charles," she said, and he jumped. When he turned to face her she could see that he'd been nearly asleep.

"Dayna," he said, like it was a nice surprise to see her standing there.

She stepped into his room, which still felt like entering a stranger's room. Old Charles had kept things neat and tidy, everything in its place. Now there was shit everywhere. Clothes all over the floor. Clean and dirty. His dresser drawers stood open, plates and bowls and sludge-filled cups balanced on his desk, on the little stool old Charles used as a nightstand, mixed in with the clothes on the floor. It even smelled different. Before it smelled of Charles's cologne threaded with weed smoke. Now it just smelled like his body, like his feet, like his breath. Baby Girl waded through the piles that made up his floor and sat on his bed, which smelled sour, like the sheets needed changing.

"Do you remember how things were before the accident?" she asked.

Charles nodded quickly, like he was proud to know the answer. "Yes, I had a whole brain and a girl I loved and fucked and guns in my pockets and everything felt heavy."

Even the old Charles wouldn't have said *A girl I fucked.* The new Charles didn't try to pretty anything up.

"Everything felt heavy?"

"Yeah, everything was on me all the time," Charles said, putting his hands on his shoulders like he was trying to protect them from the weight.

"I know what you mean," she said.

"Yes, because you're fat. I'm fat, too."

She crossed her arms over her middle, pressing them in to hide the rolls behind her T-shirt. Everywhere she went, even in her own

brother's room, she couldn't be something she wasn't. Bald. Fat. Ugly.
"That ain't a nice thing to say," she said. "Remember? You're supposed
to think how you would feel hearing something, and then if you
don't like it, then you don't say it."

"I'm fat, too," he said.

"Do you remember how you used to think? Do you remember
all the times you'd give me advice?" He could sometimes remember
things that had happened years ago better than what had happened
close to the accident or after. Part of her felt that if she just got him
to remember, if she just connected this Charles to that Charles, he'd
become whole again. Himself again.

"I remember telling you to buy your own pipe," he said, grinning.
He scooted his chair closer. "Because you never could roll blunts."

Baby Girl's heart beat fast. His smile, the way he said it, it was
him. If she ignored the basketball shorts and his fleshy torso and the
toenails he refused to trim, if she just looked at his grin and listened
to his words, it was her big brother, it was old Charles, giving her
shit like he used to. She wondered if he had to ignore her bald head,
the way she dressed, to see his little sister. *Little sister.* She hadn't felt
like the little sister in a long time.

"I could roll blunts, just not as fat as you liked them. You never
could get high off just a couple tokes." Charles picked his nose, pulled
out to study what he found. Another thing for Baby Girl to ignore.
"Do you remember what you told me after you broke up with
Crystal?"

He wiped his finger on his shorts, wagged it in her face like a scold-
ing teacher. " 'Don't give no one you ain't married to no real money.' "

" 'Twenties is fine but no more than that.' "

Charles laughed. "She was a ho, right? That's what you called her.
I remember that. Of course I do. *Of course.*"

Baby Girl could feel her throat tightening, like she might cry,
but fuck that.

"I need to ask your advice," she said. She had to force the words out. "Charles. You listening?" She felt like she was asking a kidnapper to step aside so she could speak through a peephole to the one he'd kidnapped.

He scooted his chair again. "Of course."

She heard the microwave ding. Soon Dave would be wanting them to come eat dinner. Charles heard it, too, she could tell he was trying his hardest not to leap up and go see what Dave was making. Baby Girl leaned in, holding his gaze.

"You remember that day you and your friends said you rode up on someone?"

"Of course," Charles said, but Baby Girl could tell he didn't remember all that well.

He had come home with blood on his knee, his hair matted with sweat, thick, greasy drops gliding along his jaw. Even inside, with the air-conditioning rattling away, he hadn't stopped sweating. Baby Girl had offered to get something for his knee, had asked him what happened as she daubed it with peroxide and pulled a curled stale Band-Aid across the scrape. "We all met up at the gas station," he said. "We rode up on someone and I was in front." Baby Girl had nodded like she knew what all that meant. Smoothed the blanket they draped over the rips in the couch's fabric, the once vibrant blue flowers worn and dull from being sat on over the years. Charles stared at the television. Whatever it was, he'd seemed stunned by it, frightened even. "And?" she nudged him. He'd turned, focused his eyes on hers. She felt gathered in, held tight. "I was in front," he said, like that was the end of the story.

Now Baby Girl needed him to finish the story. She pointed at his knee, at the small white scar in the shape of a fingernail. "Remember how you got that." Telling him to remember. She wasn't asking.

"Yes," Charles said. "I remember. I do. I rode my bike to the gas station to meet up with my boys." He spoke so formally now, all the swagger gone. "I had my gun in the side of my pants instead of in the back so it'd be easier to get to."

This he had never told her. "Why did you need to get to your gun easier?"

"Because we were going to ride up on someone. This boy named Bones." He stood up now, began to pace from his desk to the door, which is what new Charles did when he felt anxious. Baby Girl knew she had only so many questions left before he folded in on himself, lashed out. There was a lamp without a shade on the night-stand, and she kept her body trained toward it, ready to grab it if Charles got crazy.

"When you say you rode up on Bones, does that mean you shot him?" she asked. Dayna had been afraid to show her ignorance ask-ing a question like that, but Baby Girl didn't have that same fear, not with the Charles in front of her now.

"I was in front," he said. "I really don't like thinking about my bike." His voice was getting loud, any second Dave could rush in. And shutting the door would make him feel even more desperate, caged.

"I know," Baby Girl said quietly. "But it's 'ight, 'cause you here now with your baby sis. You ain't there, kna mean? You here." She was trying to speak to the Charles he once was, using the words he used. Trying to be a mirror that would make him become himself again.

"Okay," Charles said, and his pacing slowed. Baby Girl could feel it working.

"So you rode up on this Bones cat and what. You shot him? How you get that scrape on your knee?"

"I told you," Charles said. "I was in front. When we rode up I was supposed to shoot but I couldn't. I crashed in the yard instead."

She had wanted him to tell her sometimes people deserved it. She had wanted to hear he had done far worse. "You saying you ain't never shot no one?" she asked. She had wanted him to tell her shit like that happened every single day and people just carried on like it was nothing.

"I never shot no one," he said. "I liked riding my bike and selling stuff and helping Dave pay bills." This was another revelation, something Baby Girl had never even considered.

"You helped Dave?"

"Of course!"

A Frito-Lay truck is what had forced Charles off the road, into the guardrail and jackknifing through the air, his brain slamming against his skull even before he'd hit the ground. The doctor with the wine-colored birthmark on her neck had said all the broken bones and internal bleeding were nothing compared with what the soft meat of his brain had gone through, that even if he'd been wearing a helmet it was almost guaranteed he'd have the same brain injuries. Charles had tried to pass the truck. None of it was anyone's fault, not the truck driver's or the fuckers who built the guardrail. No one to blame, no one to ride up on.

"But you hurt people before," she said now. Her throat felt small, like it did when she was sick, like it had room for breath or words but not both.

"I don't remember," Charles said. He scooted again, put his heavy warm hands on her knees. New Charles would do that, touch her or Dave out of nowhere. The affection of a child, only since he was a man it always made Baby Girl uncomfortable. His face was oily, she could see the blackheads between his eyebrows, could see a nose hair hanging loose from his nostril. His eyes looked like they did when he was drunk, watery and bloodshot and far away, and though they were looking right into hers, they were as soulful as marbles.

Baby Girl moved her knees but his hands stayed with them, she knew he could probably feel how she no longer shaved her legs, and she was embarrassed. She had always wanted to be a baby sister he worried about, someone pretty and dumb and lusted after, not the pale, lumpy thing she was. His hands were moist, so hot they were sweating, and his breath was sharp. After their parents had died he had become a man. After Charles had his accident she had become the man. It made her flush with rage, the unfairness of it all, the mourning that never fucking stopped.

"I killed a man. I pushed him into the quarry and he died." Now her face was wet and hot, she tried to move her knees again and this time he let her, his mouth open, lower lip hanging, wet with drool. "I wanted to shoot him," she said, though she had never fully realized that until just this moment. She would have. She would have pulled the trigger. She would have gone further than Charles ever had.

"I don't like these stories," Charles said. He didn't bother wiping the drool and it hung from his chin before dropping into his lap.

"It's not a story," Baby Girl said. "I did it. I had your gun." If she could say what she had done, if she could make it real for him, maybe she could catch him up to her. Maybe that was the gap that needed the bridge.

"My gun?" He stood again, his chair toppling softly into a pile of clothes. "You killed a man?" He pushed her, hard, but she held her ground, refusing to fall back. She grabbed the lamp, yanking the cord from the wall. Held it close to her body, stood to face him.

"Calm down, Charles," she said. "Shh."

"You have to tell," Charles said. He was standing so close to her that she had to hold her head back so it wouldn't be smashed into his chest. "You have to tell!"

He was getting loud again, and this time she heard Dave call, "Everything all right back there?" She knew he'd be making his way back any second now.

Charles covered his ears, something he did when he was about to blow. The doctors said his ears would ring when he was stressed for the rest of his life. "You can't just leave him there," Charles said. "He can hear the cars going by and no one is coming to help him."

She knew he was talking about himself now. It made her feel sick, knowing he remembered lying there on the road in pain, alone. He kicked her hard in the leg. Without thinking, she brought the lamp up and around, cracking him on the cheek. He looked at her, stunned, like his ears had finally stopped ringing.

A spot of blood appeared on his cheek, a glossy dark pill. "What in God's name, Dayna!" Dave had appeared, was holding her by the arms and dragging her out of the room. Charles bent over, wailing, crying so hard that he could barely breathe. The top of his ass was out, his mouth open, crying like a toddler, he *was* a fucking retard, he was a retarded mess who would never be okay again. She ran from the sound of Charles screaming and Dave trying to soothe him, out the front door to her car. *I'm sorry. Little bitch. Cunt. Suck my dick.* Charles's brain would never heal, Jamey would never climb out of that quarry. Perry would never have half the worries Baby Girl had. *Little bitch.* Charles hadn't been who she thought he was. Neither had Jamey. Or Perry. She wouldn't be like that. She would be who she was. She would say what she did.

JIM HAD DRIVEN TO THE SCHOOL, circled its empty parking lot until a guard in a golf cart rambled over. No, he hadn't seen Perry since school let out, and he'd have known it 'cause she was quite the looker, and Jim wondered about ramming the cart with the truck, wondered was every man just a penis he had to protect Perry from, wondered if Perry was used to it, just assumed every man on earth was looking for a way to shove himself in. "No," the guard said, he hadn't run into a man fitting Jamey's description. "No, strange perverts aren't allowed on school grounds," he said, chuckling with pride. "Do me a favor," Jim said, trying to keep his voice even. "Do me a favor and get ready for me to come back here and hit you directly in your face." The guard looked insulted, but not like it was something he hadn't heard before, and drove off with a jerk.

Jim had called Jamey's parole officer after that, a woman who sounded like she had a lot bigger fish to fry. Another line rang on and on in the background as she told Jim she hadn't heard from Jamey in a few days, maybe even a week or more, but that wasn't unusual since he was only required to check in every two weeks. Did she know Jamey had been on Facebook? Did she know he'd been talking to teenaged girls? Of course she didn't know that. That was strictly forbidden, Jamey's momma was supposed to monitor his Internet usage, promised he'd only be on there to look at the news or look up a recipe.

Jim didn't know exactly why he didn't tell the P.O. he couldn't find his stepdaughter, who just happened to be one of the teenaged girls Jamey had been talking to. Maybe 'cause then it'd be real, Perry'd be missing, raped, tortured, dead. The thought made him angrier at Perry than he'd ever been before.

"Tell you what," the P.O. said. "You get me proof, concrete evidence that our man's been stepping out, and I'll be on him like a whore on a dollar."

He'd gone to a few bars, bars he knew ex-cons liked to hang out at, but these were the types of ex-cons who would eat a man like Jamey for dinner, eat his hat for dessert. Now Jim was simply driving from bus stop to bus stop. Cell phone like a hot brick in his hand. Should call the guys he knew were off-duty, see if they could be out looking too, call the cops, report her missing, call Myra. Had decided to call the P.O. back and be honest when he saw her, waiting at the number 6 transfer, sitting on the bench with her ankles together like it was any old day and she was any old teenager.

She was crying, mascara wet on her cheeks, her blouse was rumpled, her mouth looked smeared. She looked more like her momma than ever. Now he really would kill Jamey, he didn't even know he'd been considering it. He'd kill him, and he'd confess to avoid the death penalty. Neat as that.

He stopped in front of the bench. He'd been going fast and had to stomp the brake, the truck screaming. Cars behind him blew their horns, swerved around him.

"Hey," Perry said.

SHE STEPPED INTO THE TRUCK, Jim yanking her by the arm until she nearly fell into his lap.

"Where is he?" Jim's voice was low and mean.

"Who?" Perry asked. She thought of Travis, how he'd closed the door in her face, how his stuff was dried on her leg, how she smelled like sex and sweat, she smelled like the women in the jail.

"Tell me where Jamey is," Jim said. "Tell me right goddamned now."

It was like his name could stop time, could stop her heart beating, it felt like her heart and lungs were trying to work despite her quicksand blood. "Jamey?" she repeated.

"Tell me where he is so I can give his parole officer an address."

"What did Baby Girl tell you?" Perry asked. Jim was driving toward home, speeding through stop signs and running yellows. Who was waiting there for her? Baby Girl? The police?

"She told me everything," Jim said. "She told me every little last bit. So you better tell me your side."

IT HAD WORKED. Lying to Perry had worked, only she didn't tell him the story he was expecting to hear. He could smell the sickly sweet odor of sex on her, had been waiting for her to say she'd given in, or he'd forced her, or she wasn't quite sure what had happened but she'd gotten away. But instead.

"Baby Girl pushed him," Perry said. "I didn't touch him. We were trying to get him to leave us alone. He tried to get the gun and Baby Girl wasn't about to let him, and now he's at the bottom of the quarry. Dead," she added.

"The gun?" They were pulling into the trailer park now, the streetlamps dull yellow against the black sky.

"That's at the bottom of the quarry, too."

The trailers were lit up against the night, each window its own TV screen, here a show about a woman at the stove, here a show about a little boy in a cape. This was home, no place for a man like Jamey, no place for a drunk like Myra, no place for a murderer like Perry. No, not a murderer. An accessory to. They passed Jamey's trailer, the lights on but the curtains drawn, a lumpy shadow moving slowly, the TV on, not doing shit to find her son outside the confines of the trailer park. An accessory to, just as bad if not worse. Perry let it happen, didn't bother to stop it. He had planned on killing the man himself. No place for a man like Jim, either.

JIM'S HEADLIGHTS swept through the trailer, caught in Myra's eyes so two yellow dots bounced around the room everywhere she looked. She fetched Dayna a glass of water, Jim and Perry walking in just as Myra was bringing it to where the girl sat.

Myra saw that Perry had been crying. She felt how she often did in the face of her child's tears. On one side of the coin, poor thing. On the other, tough shit.

"Her daddy dropped her by," Myra said.

"Uncle," Dayna said.

"Says she needed to see you."

Perry walked over and slapped her friend, her hand landing hard on the girl's naked ear, and Myra felt pride in it, felt pride in the sureness of the hit, even as she stood to pull the girls apart, though Dayna wasn't making no move to hit back. Myra smiled, God help her, she smiled, the coin had flipped end over end and had landed right side up.

BABY GIRL HADN'T SEEN PERRY in days, but she looked different, like it had been years. Her face was gray and her hair was limp. Pretty Perry, Power Crotch Perry. Now here she was looking as old as Myra. Jamey stood behind her, soaking wet, his eyes burning into Baby Girl.

"Dayna didn't do nothing," Jim was saying. Baby Girl's ear rung, a warmth was spreading from the back of her head to her face, but it was a girly hit, not nothing to bring anyone to her knees.

"She didn't tell me about Jamey," Jim said. "You did."

Baby Girl was beginning to understand. Jim thought Perry was mad at her for snitching. But Perry had already told Jim about the quarry, it was clear, his face the color of dough. So that took care of phase one of her plan.

"We gotta make this right," she began.

"Told you what?" Myra asked.

BABY GIRL WASN'T WEARING HER LIP LINER, her lips thick and white. Her whole head was turning red, like invisible hands were choking her. A ghost's hands. Jamey.

"Make it *right*?" Perry's voice was whiny, even that was out of her control now. "*We?* I didn't do anything. You're the obsessed freak who brought the gun, you're the one who pushed him over the edge."

"No," Baby Girl said. "I didn't push him. He fell. And you're the one who didn't want to try to help him." Baby Girl was shaking her head like a wet dog. This had been her best friend. Nights on the highway in stolen cars, passing cigarettes back and forth. How? Perry wondered. This ugly thing?

"You pushed him," Perry said. "It was too late for us to do anything to help him." Perry felt wild with wanting Myra and Jim to know the truth: She hadn't killed anyone. It hadn't been her fault.

"We have to go in after him," Baby Girl said.

"What?" They all said it at once. Like some family out of a sitcom. Like some family.

BABY GIRL KNEW it wouldn't go over easy. Knew she'd have to be persuasive. Dangle a blood-soaked cutlet in front of old Baby Girl's nose. So she pulled out the knife, Charles's favorite knife because of the way it glinted, the one she had to hide from him under the box of crackers on a shelf way up high.

In the car on the way to Perry's she'd rolled her window down. Let the air and the smells come in. A baptism of exhaust or some shit. Dave would be proud of her, and so would Charles. Eye for an eye.

"What?" Perry, Myra, and Jim, all at once. Like actors in the kind of shit program Charles would watch.

"We're going in after him, Perry." Baby Girl held the knife out like it was a sword. Aimed at all of them. "We'll jump in and get him out and bring him to wherever you bring someone you murdered." She walked toward Perry, holding the knife like a finger pointing her out. "We'll say what we did."

She could see the way Myra was looking at Jim, like, *Pull your gun, dumbass*, and Jim's hand was curling, his arm bending, he was definitely reaching for it.

THE GUN WAS IN THE TRUCK. In its holster under the front seat. Jim had put it there when he'd set out to find Perry. Had forgotten it in his rush to get her inside. Dayna's hand was shaking but her grip was strong. He didn't think she wanted to hurt no one but knew she would if he came near. He kept going for the gun, though, all muscle memory, maybe she'd think he had it on him, maybe she'd put down the knife, maybe she'd calm down when he told her he wasn't about to have either of them confess to anyone.

The doorbell rang, and he flinched, hard enough to be embarrassed if he'd done it in front of the guys at the jail.

MYRA COULD SEE JAMEY'S MOTHER out the screen door, holding her cane at her side.

"My boy served his time," the woman said. "And I want you to hand him over."

"Jesus Christ," Myra started to say, but the woman raised her stake, and Myra got a better look at it, not a cane at all, actually. It was a gun, though Myra couldn't tell if it was the BB gun Jamey had with him that first night, the night she'd met Pete, or a real gun.

"Those are just BBs," Myra said, flapping her hand to dismiss it all. She wanted everyone to believe it, even Lulu. "My daddy used to shoot the stray cats up with BBs back home. Not one of them seemed to give a damn aside from a limp or a busted tail. Go on and shoot."

The woman did, one-armed, the other arm bracing her on the stair railing. The whole screen came away, Myra watching the pane fall in and land on the dingy old rag rug she'd had at the front door forever and a day. Those weren't no BBs. This was a shotgun, Myra almost shouted it. *A shotgun!* Like she'd gotten the answer right on some game show. The woman shot again.

IT WAS A RELIEF, the sting that soon became a second kind of skin, skin that was all open nerves and pain and blood. Pain was a relief. It let her drop the knife, it let her go to her knees, it let her forgive them for looking at her like a dying dog instead of the human girl she was. That explosion was a bullet? Two bullets. Like they were trying to nail her shirt good and snug to her chest. Her head still intact, though. She'd be all right. She'd have done her eye for an eye without ever setting foot in that quarry. Jamey backed out the door, backed right through his momma. Ha-ha, there never was no Jamey, she always knew that. *I've been shot!* is what people said on TV. Funny thing to say when it's so obvious. Her blood like burbling warm mud. She wondered could she pop out the bullets from her chest like you popped a zit. Charles would know. He'd pop it for her. Charles was her brother, Dave was her uncle, she had people. "Shit, she's all white," she heard someone say, though it sounded like a like a like a robot, the voice all buzz. Myra's lips were moving, must have been her. Perry had her mouth open, wide enough to be screaming, though Baby Girl couldn't hear no screaming. What was wrong with her ears? She was wrong. Perry was still pretty. Perry would always be pretty. She wished she'd stabbed her a little with the knife. *I'ma get mine.* Why weren't they calling someone? She was sinking, kind of. The floor was opening up, kind of. She was wrong, those bullets weren't no joke. She lay down. Better. *Hey,* she tried to say. *That fat thing was Jamey's momma? Poor Jamey,* she thought, the highway empty before her, the sky a navy quilt. She pushed down on the gas. She was on her way to Charles, had to get him before that balloon got too swole. She'd save him. She'd become him. His gun his knife his bald head, only she'd go further than he ever had, 'cause this was her car. It was her car this time.

Acknowledgments

I began as a poet, pretended to write a novel in grad school, then found my home in flash fiction. Being granted the opportunity to write this novel is a gift I can never adequately repay, and I am in debt to the following wonderful people:

Emily Bell, bravest editor, who believed in me before I ever wrote the first word in this book.

Jim Rutman, who read a tiny sliver and still wanted to be my agent.

Sarah Rose Etter, an amazing friend and writer whose feedback and support made me feel less afraid.

Zach Dodson, because it all started with you, bro.

Matt Trupia, who talked me off the ledge many times.

Brian and Traci Knudson and Chad Chmielowicz, who let me take the time I needed away from work in order to focus on my writing.

My parents, whose love of reading and writing made me who I am, and who love me despite the fact that I don't write about baskets of puppies or happy birthday parties.

My son, Parker. I live my life to make you proud.

And finally, my brilliant, beloved husband, Ben Lyon, who makes all my dreams come true.